THE TWIN PAINTINGS MYSTERY

LR Walker

Published in the United States of America, 2017
Newtonia Publishing LLC
300 Lenora Street #153 Seattle WA 98121
newtoniapublishing@gmail.com

ISBN-13: 9780692867433 (Newtonia Publishing LLC)
ISBN-10: 0692867430

Library of Congress Control Number: 2017904944
Newtonia Publishing LLC, Seattle, WA

Other books by LR Walker:
Nonfiction
The Mystery of Garabandal: Fantasy or Fraud? Ghost or God?

For my mother, with love

ACKNOWLEDGMENTS

Deep thanks and appreciation to readers who provided feedback on this book, especially Deborah Clarke, Christa Colouzis, Katherine Jenkins and Joyce Walker.

CHAPTER 1

SATANIC CHRISTMAS

Cornelia had been lost in Asia so long, she'd completely forgotten about the Satanic Christmas.

She saw it the first time at the age of ten in the small town of Newton, Missouri. Cornelia's grandmother had taken her across the road to visit her neighbor, Miss Grace. Despite being friends, Cornelia's grandmother disapproved of Miss Grace because Miss Grace accepted "commodities," which Cornelia understood to be some sort of government handout in the form of canned goods. But that was nothing compared to how scandalized her grandmother was by Miss Grace's paintings.

"What is it?" Cornelia asked as she stared, mesmerized, at the chaotic carnival scene displayed before her. At the age of ten, Cornelia had been undersized, smiling, and pony-tailed, with warm brown eyes. Her white-blonde hair was offset by the only trait she'd inherited from her grandmother—expressive dark eyebrows that cast a slight shadow on an otherwise sunny countenance.

"I call it "The Satanic Christmas," Miss Grace calmly explained. Miss Grace was frail as a sparrow, with a tiny voice and a cloud of silver hair. "You know where it's from, don't you?"

"Of course she doesn't know where it's from," Grandmother, tall and stern-faced, retorted.

"Where is it from?" Cornelia asked.

"It's from the future," her grandmother dourly replied.

Now, almost twenty years later, Cornelia stood on a clogged and buckled sidewalk on touristy Silom Road in Bangkok, Thailand and stared through a plate-glass window at Miss Grace's *Satanic Christmas*. The shop window was crowded with silk paintings of shimmering rice paddies, and sandalwood carvings of gaunt, serene Buddhas, and royal Thai marionettes that dangled, limbs contorted, in the dusty light. Cornelia saw her own wavering reflection in the glass, the blonde ponytail long gone, replaced by short, sleek, almost-white hair that never troubled her in the humidity and heat. She was still undersized, but her perpetual smile—something she'd inherited from her father—was gone, displaced temporarily by shock.

Cornelia stared past herself, into the midst of a dark Thai shop crammed with Oriental relics, both sacred and profane. Here, in a country where Christmas wasn't even a holiday and three-headed serpents were sacred, glowed a baffling and thoroughly American painting: "Satanic Christmas." A customer brushed past her and pushed open the door of the shop, setting off a tinkling bell and releasing a blast of artificially icy air. It was as if a false Christmas were being celebrated inside, off-key and out-of-sight.

Cornelia had already heard that Miss Grace, in the intervening years, had become something of a sensation. Miss Grace had to be quite aged by now—she'd been no spring chicken even then. A folk artist, they called her. Southern folk. American folk. A visionary artist, an *outsider*. There were numerous labels, but none of them quite captured the unsettling apocalyptic images that geysered forth from these self-taught, so-called "backwoods" American artists. The artists were off the beaten path, lost in the woods and hills of red-clayed, red-state America, without MFAs or even an education. They were quaint cultural artifacts to be studied and written up in a journal somewhere, and subsequently featured on NPR or PBS. It was remarkable enough that their paintings had journeyed into the limelight of Manhattan. But Cornelia could not for the life of her imagine how one of them had snaked its way half-way round the world and ended up here. How she and the painting had *both* ended up here.

Her grandmother had been gone five years. It was the event of Grandmother's death that had catapulted Cornelia away from home. Cornelia's single deep root to her own home was severed. Her childhood had been anchored to her grandmother after both her parents died in a car accident. With her grandmother's death, she had no anchor—so Cornelia, always light on her feet in ballet and gymnastics as a child, spun away in a dizzying new direction. She lost herself in the heat and rats and rice and spice of a surreal, askew Bangkok slum which had sprung up along the waterfront in the shadow of massive shipyard cranes which loaded and unloaded container ships. The slum was a labyrinth of tangled pathways and it vibrated with a twisted power that left her disoriented. She frequently got lost in there, and sometimes she had trouble walking upright—although maybe it was because of the ramshackle wooden walkways built haphazardly above contaminated waters. On the surface, the misery seemed mystical—how else to explain it? But scratch the surface and there were no strange magnetic forces at work—just all-too-human forces generating intractable problems.

Christians eked out a living butchering pigs in one corner of the slum because the Muslim and Buddhist slum-dwellers—on either side—refused for the sake of religion. But when it came to learning English, the slum was practical and ecumenical. Cornelia taught all faiths—Buddhist, Hindu, Muslim, Christian—and even, depending on who drifted in, numerous nationalities—Thais, Cambodians, Burmese, Laotians. Sometimes she felt like the Good

Witch Glenda, who descended into the fetid alleyways of the slum to sprinkle fairy dust and confer upon the downtrodden inhabitants what they hoped was their golden ticket out of hell: *fluent English*. They all looked up longingly, hoping she could zap this international language of wealth and commerce right into them.

"*Yim su-eye,*" they said as Cornelia approached. Beautiful smile.

But the smiling Good Witch Glenda hadn't been able to get her act together when it really mattered. She'd been useless when it came to getting the ruby slippers off Dorothy. Dorothy was stuck with them. In Cornelia's experience, English didn't get zapped into anyone and misery didn't get zapped out. English leaked with agonizing slowness into her students like an I.V. drip. Possibly it was because her slum-dwelling students were often busy with other things. Some of them might be busy battling AIDS, while others might be feeding themselves by selling flowers to predatory pedophiles. Some might spend their days begging in the heat and turning the proceeds over to their "handlers." Mostly, they were just busy being among the poorest of the earth and working themselves to death in the process. Whatever religion, whatever nationality—they had precious little time to learn their English vowels.

But Cornelia had tried to teach them anyway, and had lost herself in the slum in the process. She had fallen in love with her students, who were alternately passionate and apathetic about learning English, depending on whether they'd been evicted from their squatter's shack that day or had spent the night before in a government emergency room coughing up blood. They were caught in such a daily maelstrom that Cornelia admired them greatly for trying to learn English at all. Why even bother? But for some reason, they did. Chanya, the director of the program where Cornelia taught, said learning English gave them hope. English was like a religion they were desperately trying to convert to because it promised an afterlife—life after the slums. Whatever their mysterious motives, they labored mightily to master the future perfect verb tense when in the continuous present a whirlpool of wretchedness threatened to suck them down for good. For that reason, Cornelia couldn't pull herself away. In the process, she conveniently forgot about her grief, her past, and even her future.

Until now.

Astonished, she practically pressed her face against the storefront glass. It couldn't really be *Satanic Christmas*. The painting was completely out of place here. It was from the American boondocks. Naïve, primitive, insular. It sprang from a world that barely existed anymore, anywhere. And this was the throbbing heart of metropolitan Asia. Sleek, crowded, criminal. Bangkok was every modern, developing city, only more so.

But Asia had abruptly vanished. Cornelia was ten years old again. She could no longer smell the spicy green chicken curry that bubbled in a vat in a nearby sidewalk stall. She could no longer hear hundreds of motorcycle taxis buzzing like a horde of angry bees down the street. Bangkok—that vibrant collision of seductive Old Siam with brute-force industrialization—went sullenly black-and-white. It muted. And Cornelia was like one of those puppets, suspended helplessly in a vacuum.

Riveted by *Satanic Christmas*. The canvas seemed barely able to contain its power, warped by the heat of a dangerous meaning. She couldn't bear to take it seriously, this crude, psychedelic warning from the Book of Revelation, brush-stroked into life by an ancient, ditzy Southern lady. But she also couldn't tear her eyes away.

They Will Gloat and Exchange Gifts With Glee Once the Two Witnesses Are Dead.

That's what Miss Grace had painted across the bottom of *Satanic Christmas*.

"Who are the two witnesses?" Cornelia had shyly asked eighteen years earlier.

Miss Grace stopped acting fluttery and gave her a piercing look, then focused her watery blue eyes with grave intensity on her grandmother. "Do you read this child the Bible?"

"I do," Grandma said sharply. "But not that part. That part's too scary for a child."

"Well, don't you think she, of all people, needs to know who the Two Witnesses are?" Miss Grace continued somberly.

"What part's scary?" Cornelia persisted, all ears. "What do I need to know?"

"You ask your grandma to read this story from the Book of Revelation to you tonight," Miss Grace replied, waving nonchalantly at her traumatic, dramatic painting. "Tell her not to skip the scariest parts." Diminutive Miss Grace peered threateningly over her bifocals at Cornelia's grandmother.

Eighteen years later, Cornelia stood on the sidewalk in Bangkok, and she smelled the frying bacon and bubbling gravy in Miss Grace's kitchen. She heard the chickens clucking pleasantly through her screen door. She smelled the rich, dark clods of earth recently upturned in Miss Grace's garden. And in the painting before her, she saw again the menacing parts that delicate Miss Grace had refused to censor.

CHAPTER 2
THE SLUM

Cornelia stared at *Satanic Christmas* hanging in that shop window, and she suddenly, desperately wanted to get home for Christmas. She wanted snow and Christmas trees and red and green lights and bells and carols. She felt like this bleak vision from home had found its way to her deliberately—it was from her grandmother, it was from Miss Grace, it was from the past, it was from America—all reaching out to Cornelia, calling her urgently home.

"I will be back soon," she promised Chanya. He was un-used to anyone staying five weeks, much less five years. English teaching in locales that were difficult and off-the-beaten-path attracted the young and idealistic, the generous and adventurous, the criminal and lost. But it attracted none of them for very long. Chanya gripped Cornelia's hand and spoke fervently to her.

"*Tong klaap,*" he said. Then he repeated himself, with great desperation, in English. "You *must* come back here."

"I *will,*" Cornelia promised. She could feel his blood beating in his clenched palm. His hand was strong and warm. "*Yawk klaap,*" Cornelia insisted. I *want* to return."

"I'm afraid I will drink too much while you are gone," Chanya lamented. "I can't bear it here alone. It is breaking my heart."

This was true. He wept easily while drinking Chang beer and eating grilled meat on hot nights at sidewalk restaurants. As he wept and sweated from spice and heat and sorrow, his skin took on a burnished glow. He would abruptly break into full-hearted laughter. He was smooth-skinned, as many Thai men seemed to be, and he was short, though taller than Cornelia. But Chanya was also stocky—not so Thai—and hot-hearted, not Thai at all. He was the opposite of *jai yen,* or cool-hearted, which was the Thai ideal. *Jai yen yen,* Thais would calmly murmur when overwrought Westerners lost their cool. *Keep a cool heart,* or as Cornelia preferred to translate, Keep a cool head. If Chanya saw trouble in the slum, he was likely as not to wade right into it without a second thought. This did not set well with certain unsavory slum elements, as Cornelia constantly reminded Chanya. But despite his Thai nationality and Buddhist faith, Chanya wore his passion on his hardworking, sweat-soaked sleeve.

Chanya and Cornelia often commiserated late into the night over the daily tragedies they'd seen, Chanya giving Cornelia pointers on speaking Thai, while Cornelia cooked up miraculous new models of English-teaching which would save the world. The next morning Cornelia's bright ideas never seemed as lustrous, nor her Thai as fluent, but they had talked each other through another long evening, and they were each able to virtuously go home alone and sleep—Cornelia to her studio on the edge of the slum, Chanya to the cot in the backroom of his slum office. Chanya had confided to Cornelia—much to her alarm—that before she'd come, he'd often gone home alone and drunk himself to sleep. The twenty-something teachers who came and went as they backpacked their way around the world in search of adventure were of little solace to him. Cornelia had arrived and then stayed, and that had made all the difference. Of course, she was able to stay so long in an invisible, low-paying job because she had received a modest inheritance from her grandmother that went much further in Thailand than in the United States. She called it "modest," but the heft of it had surprised her. Cornelia had never understood where her grandmother's money had come from—from saving her pitiful social security check, or from selling her organic, free-range eggs before anyone knew what free-range was?

"You talk about my passion, but if I hide it, it burns me, and so I drink to put out the flames," Chanya pronounced poetically. "When I don't drink, the fire flickers into a roar that I can't contain. This is what you hear and see. It's only because you have shared it with me that I have been able to bear the flame's heat. Once you leave, I will drink and fall silent again." He studied Cornelia with great tenderness. "When you smile, you radiate...something. I can't put my finger on. Not just sweetness. Sweet mixed with spice. Sugar and chili peppers. Some salt and fermentation. Fresh and pungent, like cilantro or basil." He paused, considering. "And you are so small." He frowned slightly. "Who is it who hides in that locket next to your heart?"

"It's my father," Cornelia explained, touching the silver locket she always wore. "A picture of my father." Cornelia got her endearing smile and last name—Small—from her father. But she got her petite stature, fair hair, sympathetic brown eyes and poise from her quiet and mysterious mother.

"This slum breaks your heart, but it has healed mine." As soon as Cornelia said the words, she realized they were true. "I won't forget that. I promise I'll return," she reiterated.

"I know you will," Chanya said, and smiled slyly. "Because I have your precious painting."

CHAPTER 3
THE PAINTING

Her precious painting. This is how she got it.

Cornelia stepped from the blazing brightness of Silom Road into the hushed darkness of the artifacts shop. A small neon sign buzzed in the window, touting the shop's name: *The Secret Value*. Maybe the name had become muddied in translation. When Thai stores catered to foreigners, as they did in this part of Bangkok, odd juxtapositions of English sometimes resulted. Maybe the intended meaning was something like *Hidden Bargains*. But Cornelia liked *The Secret Value* better. It did indeed get her attention. She braced herself as she paused beside the painting. She didn't want the shop owner to know she was desperate to buy it. She was hoping the Thai store owner would have no clue that he had genuine American artwork on his hands. A plot had already sprung to life in Cornelia's mind. She had tried to develop her bargaining muscle after five years as a foreigner shopping in Thai markets. They often assumed she had money and tried to overcharge her, and she had tried to learn how to pay less. The key was to persevere in a polite way.

"May I help you?" a male voice asked in a perfect American accent.

Cornelia jumped. She squinted into the dim shop where a young Thai man stood casually behind the counter. "You speak English," she remarked, trying to hide her dismay. She felt disoriented now by the darkness and the American accent and the painting that shone malevolently in the window. Her confidence in her ability to connive was already dissolving. *Keep walking and the sea always parts,* grandmother had often commanded Cornelia. Her grandmother had seemed to will away obstacles and difficulties by glowering at the future, daring it to stand in her way. Cornelia's pleasing temperament had absorbed the same philosophy and produced the opposite effect: instead of using fierceness, Cornelia disarmed difficulties with a smile. And in truth, when she smiled, the sea often parted. Her smile seemed to have a mysterious and magical effect. Or maybe it wasn't magic—maybe her friendly expression simply put others at ease. Her petite build was also more likely to trigger protectiveness than aggression in people. There was yet another possibility. Cornelia's one fierce feature—her dramatic dark eyebrows—hinted at something hidden and unpredictable, which left her disarmed protectors slightly unsettled. Besides, Cornelia's slender arms and legs were noticeably muscled, through no particular effort of her own. This suggested a surprising strength undergirded Cornelia's soft, feminine demeanor, a concealed power which might have left others off-balance without knowing why. Although right now, it was Cornelia who felt off-balance. The clerk behind the counter merely appeared bored.

"I speak English because I'm an American," he said. "I'm just getting to know my relatives. Spending some time here."

"Oh," Cornelia said, heart thudding. "Well, that explains it."

"Can I help you with something?" he asked, drumming his fingertips lightly on the countertop. "I mean, are you looking for something special?" A portrait of the King of Thailand hung behind him, and a shrine to a revered Buddhist monk sat at one end of the counter. Incense spiraled lazily in front of the shrine, which was decorated with a wilting jasmine wreath. Cornelia also noticed a cup of water and a small offering of sticky rice, coconut milk and mango before the shrine.

"Well," she replied, suddenly remembering her plan. "Do you sell any gems?"

The man frowned slightly.

"No, not really," he admitted. "Some fake stuff, cheap jade bracelets, that kind of thing. Nothing of value, though. You know, there are lots of places that sell gems. I can point you in the right direction."

"Oh, that would be great. I just want to pick a few things up before I go home," Cornelia lied. She realized she was fingering the oval locket which she wore around her neck, something she always did when she was nervous. The silver locket was from her grandmother.

"No problem," the young Thai-American said agreeably. "I'll write down a few places for you. They aren't far." In good Samaritan mode, he bent over and began scratching swiftly on a pad.

Ever so casually, Cornelia sauntered over to the painting.

"Huh!" she exclaimed, trying to feign surprise.

The clerk looked up from his scribbling.

"Isn't that strange!" she added, staring hard at the paint-ing now. "I mean, in a place like this. It doesn't look Thai. It looks—American."

"It *is* American," the clerk said. He grinned and looked very young. He was college-age, maybe, but just barely. "Not Thai."

"Obviously," Cornelia agreed. "Well, isn't that something. American. Not Thai. What's it doing here?"

Did something flicker in the clerk's eyes, a shift from casual to alert? Or did Cornelia imagine it?

"Some American guy sold it to us. He said he had a Thai wife and had been living upcountry for years. Anyway, his wife died and he was headed back to America. Needed to raise some cash to get there. Had a lot of medical debt from his wife's illness. In fact, he brought in a bunch of gems and my uncle sent him off on his merry way with those. That's how I know where the gem shops are. My uncle figured they were smuggled in from Burma and he doesn't deal in gems anyway. But my uncle liked the guy because he spoke perfect Thai, and he felt sorry about the guy's hard-luck story, so he took the painting. My uncle thought it was pretty out-of-place here, but I told him it might catch some foreigners' eyes as they walk by. He figured foreign tourists would be looking for exotic Asian, not American. But it caught your eye. So maybe I was right." The young Thai was watching Cornelia now with obvious interest. Cornelia briefly considered the possibility that this young man could see straight through her, that he knew that the painting was what she'd wanted all along. But it wouldn't do to psyche herself out. She smiled at the clerk.

"Do you want it?" he asked.

"Want what?" Cornelia asked, wary.

"The painting," he replied.

"Oh," she laughed. This was the explanation for the college student's sudden scrutiny. He realized he could make a sale. Why had she been so paranoid, anyway? Still smiling, she bit her tongue so as not to cry out, "Yes! I want it! It's my childhood! It's my grandmother! It's Miss Grace! It's mine!" Instead she shrugged. "I don't know. It would be a conversation piece, I guess. 'Hey, everyone, look at what I picked up in Thailand! A piece of pure Americana!' Everyone would get a kick out of that. How much is it? I mean, it's not even real art or anything, is it? It looks—cartoonish." She felt sly and triumphant. She was going to get this painting for a pittance.

"Well, it looks pretty goofy," he agreed. "*Satanic Christmas*. It sounds like a heavy metal album. But there was some woman asking about it just an hour or so ago. An American woman, just like you," he offered. "I mean, she was older than you. Gray-haired.

And she told me she lives here. She's married to some Thai guy. She said she was a volunteer or something years ago and she fell in love with the Thai guy and never left. Anyway, she just saw the painting when she was walking by and she came right in. She kept saying, "Where did you get this? I've never seen anything like this in Thailand before!" I told her we buy all of our stuff from wholesalers, that I didn't know where exactly, but my uncle would know if she wanted to come back." He laughed. "I didn't want to tell her the truth, because I started worrying it was stolen or something. I didn't really expect the painting to attract so much attention so fast, and I didn't want my uncle to get in any trouble on my watch. After all, putting the painting in the window was my idea. If she'd been a tourist, I wouldn't have worried. But since she's married to a Thai, that made me nervous. I worried they could recognize stolen art and report it, whereas a tourist couldn't—or wouldn't care even if they did think it was stolen. You know, just passing through." He frowned. "Something else bothered me. She kept asking if I knew the painting's *provenance*—you know, who all owned it before. The way she was asking made me nervous. Almost like she suspected it was stolen. Or that she was going to check on it, for sure." The store employee shook his head. "But this lady said she was definitely interested in buying it, so I told her my uncle handled all the art sales." He chuckled. "I just made that up on the spot. I told her to come back later today and she could talk to my uncle about the whole thing. I figured he could make his own decision about her, whether he wanted to deal with her. He likes to keep things clean. I told you how he was about the gems. Then the lady said she just wanted the painting because it reminded her of home." He scowled and shook his head. "*Home.* I'm so sure. It doesn't remind me anything about home. Of course I'm from L.A. Does it remind you of home?"

Cornelia swallowed and lied. "Not really, no."

He shrugged. "Anyway, she said she'd come back and bring her husband. They might want it for their *collection*." He paused, to let that little tidbit sink in. "She didn't even ask about a price," he added, for effect.

Cornelia's heart sank. She had thought she was going to come in here and hustle this guy. Why did she suddenly feel like she was the one being hustled? If an American art-collector was on the trail of this painting, she'd never be able to afford it. She felt sick, as if she were losing her grandmother, her home, and her past all over again. *Your grandmother would never approve of this defeatist attitude.* The stern voice inside brought an instant smile to Cornelia's face. Cornelia had never heard a stern voice *inside* until her Grandmother died. She seemed to have found a way to live on, browbeating Cornelia forever. Cornelia raised her face and looked at the boy.

"On the other hand," he remarked thoughtfully, and Cornelia could see his gears churning. He was thinking, *what if the picture was stolen?* He had enough sense to know an actual sale in the next few minutes from a passing tourist was safer for his uncle than waiting on a savvy art-collector with a Thai husband who might spell trouble for his uncle's shop. Besides, who knew if she'd even return for this weird, garish picture once she'd had a chance to reconsider? It might be better to be rid of the thing as quickly as possible. His uncle wasn't running a gem shop, and he wasn't running an art gallery, either. Just a touristy trinket shop. A bird in hand, as they say. Cornelia was the bird.

"How about a thousand dollars?" he asked.

Cornelia didn't blink and didn't look away. She stood, slight, quiet, tranquil. She smiled. She hoped her face radiated certainty and that her eyebrows, which sometimes had a mind of their own, didn't betray her inner turmoil.

The store assistant sounded defensive. "My uncle paid the American man five hundred for it, but only because he showed us the *Miss Grace Series* on the internet. The seller pointed out that those prices were a lot higher than $500 and we were getting a steal. Plus, there's no image of *Satanic Christmas* on the internet. The website said hardly anyone has ever seen it, that no one is sure it even really exists. The artist never put it up for sale. A journalist claimed to get a glimpse of it once when he was interviewing the painter. It was just a rumor, really." The young store assistant cocked his head. "That painting could be worth a lot more than we realize. So you're getting a steal, too."

"If it's genuine," Cornelia countered, even though she knew it was.

"That's what I said," the store clerk admitted. "I thought the seller might just be some American scam artist passing off fake work from artists he found on the internet. After all, it's easy to call this painting *Satanic Christmas* if no one's ever seen the real *Satanic Christmas*. And if the painting was an original, I wondered why he didn't take it back to America with him and sell it for a lot more. But he said he was short on cash, and—" Here, he hesitated.

"And what?" Cornelia prompted.

"He seemed nervous, which made me wonder if it *was* stolen," he confessed. "Like maybe he was afraid he'd get caught if he tried to take it out of the country. And he even seemed a little scared." The clerk sounded puzzled. "As if—maybe someone was after him." He looked up at Cornelia, realizing belatedly he'd said too much. "But I don't think it's stolen," he hastened to add. "No police or anyone like that has come around asking questions. Just an American art collector," he added meaningfully.

The Thai-American clerk had hustled her. He'd known all along the painting might have value. One thousand dollars. A huge sale for a trinket shop like this, where most items went for five bucks if they were lucky. And Cornelia was desperate to have it immediately, spooked into action by the ghost of the other "American lady," the mysterious art collector. But a thousand dollars was an enormous bite out of her bank account. She lived off her inheritance by placing herself on a strict monthly budget and because the dollar went a long way in Thailand. She hated to bust her budget unless absolutely necessary. This was absolutely necessary.

"Six hundred," she countered.

The clerk guffawed. "Eight hundred."

"Seven."

The young man grimaced and met her gaze. "How about seven hundred fifty?"

Cornelia didn't care if it was stolen or not. It was, she felt in her bones, *her* painting. She pulled out her credit card without missing a beat.

The salesclerk wrapped it up in brown paper and put it in a black plastic sack for her. Cornelia was so euphoric she could barely contain herself, but as she started to turn away, the chatty young Thai-American, who had obviously been starving to speak English to someone, offered her one final morsel.

"You know, there's a twin," he said.

"What do you mean?" Cornelia asked.

"The guy who sold it to me. He said, "I wish I had the twin to this painting. I could have doubled my money."

"Where is it?" Cornelia asked.

"That's exactly what I asked," he said eagerly. "And the guy said, "I don't know. But I'm going to find out. I know some people who are looking real hard for that twin. And I need the cash."

"That's interesting," Cornelia said slowly. She had no idea what "twin painting" he was talking about, but she knew exactly where it might be. "Who's looking so hard for it, anyway?" she added.

The shop assistant grinned. "Don't know. Sure does seem like a lot of people are interested in such an ugly painting. But you're the one who got it. Lucky you."

"Lucky me," Cornelia echoed. She shivered slightly in the air conditioned shop, eager to step outside into the sun.

CHAPTER 4

INTO THE VOID

All around Cornelia, passengers were dozing through the night. They had hurtled over Vietnam and Manila and not even known it. They'd passed over Taipei and the Ryuku Islands, careened over China and Japan at 39,000 feet and 555 miles per hour, and now they were crossing 6000 miles of nothing but sea. She looked out into the darkness where the air temperature this high was minus 58 degrees. Bangkok and Tokyo and Hong Kong had disappeared beneath swirling mists like a land of dreams. Cornelia remembered the first time she had flown into Thailand. As they descended, it sparkled green and pristine below her, the glittering blue-green sea lapping affectionately at its edges. It looked resplendent. When Cornelia had stepped out of the airport, she'd been socked in the face by a suffocating blanket of humidity, jasmine and sewage that kept her off-balance for much of her time there. She never knew what to expect from Thailand. It surprised her at every turn, at once seductive and punishing. Now she had left the spicy heat of the slum and the spunky children and passionate Chanya far behind, and she was shooting like a star into a black and frozen void.

She wished Chanya were hurtling along beside her. She wished his dark, oversized hand were squeezing her small, pale one, as it had done just before she'd left, when he'd made her promise to return. He had begged her to return in time for a ceremony he'd just been invited to, honoring his work with the children in the slums. He promised to text her with the date and details as soon as he knew them. Cornelia swore she would return in time.

She closed her hand and made a fist and sighed. Then she turned away from the black void and stared again into the equally intimidating *Satanic Christmas.* It was just an image stored on her phone, of course, lit feebly by her overhead reading light. Cornelia had left the real painting, clunky and awkward in its heavy frame, with Chanya. Chanya had demanded it as insurance that she'd return to Thailand. After only a moment's thought, she'd agreed. She had no home left in the U.S. She had no place to bring the painting to. What if it were damaged in transit, or customs officials gave her trouble? The painting appeared vulnerable to Cornelia, fragile as a memory, and she felt fiercely protective of it. She had re-gained those lost nights with her grandmother, nights when she had nestled beneath her quilts while her grandmother had read to her from the Bible, and Cornelia was never going to lose them again. She had conveniently misplaced a lot of memories, she now realized, while she'd kept herself preoccupied with the squalid razzle-dazzle of the slums.

But the painting had delivered its unsettling message to her, loud and clear: *Go home.* She didn't know why she needed to go home, but she felt like she was being summoned. Perhaps Miss Grace had reached out to her across the years and the miles. Perhaps she had something urgent to say to Cornelia. But for heaven's sake, what? Cornelia studied the photograph.

In *Satanic Christmas,* it was as if Miss Grace had taken an image of the warmest, most nostalgic Christmas past and plunged it into acid first, and then a furnace. The painting was warped and discolored, as if it had gone through hell. At first glance, the painting seemed not so much black-and-white as gray. Most of the color had been bled dry, except for sinister splotches of dark red and sticky black. Like much "outsider art", the painting was very busy—it would take Cornelia hours to comb through all the images Miss Grace had depicted. One figure in the painting—it was hard to say if he was a man because he was visible only from the back—was huge and muscled and naked, throwing scalding lava into a woman's face. Someone else was descending upside down wearing a pale olive-green cape, his face beet-red. In the background, men, women, and—most disturbingly—children were exchanging huge wrapped gifts. The gifts, Cornelia realized, were the dark red and black splotches. The people trading presents were at first laughing. But as she continued to stare, the humans seemed to shrivel and shriek. It was almost as if she could hear them screaming. The painting didn't seem static—it somehow managed to torture *all* the senses. And in keeping with the style of outsider art, images were not all that Miss Grace had used to convey her eerie message. She had written in cramped black old-fashioned script in every nook and cranny of the painting. In some places, the writing started out large and gradually shrank smaller and smaller until it was impossible to read. Cornelia realized she'd need a magnifying glass to read the tiniest writing. But some of it was scripture, and instantly recognizable to her from her childhood.

Men out of every people, race, language and nation will stare at their corpses, for three-and-a-half days, not letting them be buried, and the people of the world will be glad about it and celebrate the event by giving presents to each other, because these two prophets have been a plague to the people of the world.

The image of the painting was small on her phone screen, but Cornelia noticed some kind of border had been painted around the four edges of the painting, framing it. All the chaos and carnage, in words and images, took place within this border. The only thing outside the border, in fact, was a small crucifix at the very bottom of the painting, in the center. Miss Grace was a Pentecostal lady preacher—not a Catholic. Why had she painted a crucifix on her painting? *Men of every people, race, language and nation will stare at their corpses for three-and-a-half days.* Whose corpses were being broadcast on TV and computer screens across the globe? Who were the two prophets lying dead in those streets? And whose death could inspire so much glee, but also trigger doom? Who *were* the two witnesses?

After the three-and-a-half days, God breathed life into them and they stood up, and everybody who saw it happen was terrified; then they heard a loud voice from heaven say to them, "Come up here", and while their enemies were watching, they went up to heaven in a cloud. Immediately, there was a violent earthquake, and a tenth of the city collapsed; seven thousand persons were killed in the earthquake, and the survivors, overcome with fear, could only praise the God of heaven.

"Look at yourself," a chiding voice in Cornelia's head said. "You got on an airplane because of a far-fetched prophecy and an absurd painting, for God's sake. You left behind your work, the students you love, the blazing hot intensity of life in the slum. You left behind long, beer-soaked conversations late into the night with Chanya. You left behind—"

"Shut up," Cornelia muttered, and the man next to her glanced cautiously at her, then quickly looked away. Cornelia sighed. She couldn't help it. One look at *Satanic Christmas* and her ten-year-old self had sprung back to life: the ponytail was swinging, her eyebrows were slashes of consternation, and she was longing for answers. The main question in her young heart had been: But is the painting *true*? Are the Two Witnesses *coming*? And if it's true, *who* are the Two Witnesses? *Where* are the Two Witnesses?

Cornelia just never expected, eighteen years later, to find herself wondering the exact same thing. She couldn't wait to see Miss Grace, to see the surprise on her face when Cornelia showed up at her door, to tell Miss Grace that she'd found *Satanic Christmas,* and in the Orient, of all places—and that Cornelia's entire childhood had come rushing back to her. If Miss Grace wanted her painting back, Chanya would ship it immediately. Maybe that's what this was all about. Miss Grace had lost her painting, and serendipity— God? Fate?—was bringing it back to her, via Cornelia.

Besides all that, there was the American man who had sold *Satanic Christmas* to the Bangkok shop, the one who was interested in tracking down Miss Grace and the "twin painting." Cornelia wanted to tell Miss Grace this man might show up at her door one day, wanting to buy another painting. She wanted Miss Grace to get her money's worth and not be taken advantage of—Miss Grace was old now, and Cornelia had no idea if her health were frail, or her mind feeble.

Cornelia had also completely forgotten about Miss Grace's voice, but she would hear it again soon.

She stepped off a Thai jet into an American airport where Christmas, she discovered, was gone. The airport, aflame with the seemingly uncontainable controversy of Christmas, had stripped itself of any vestige of that blasphemous holiday. Even bland and cheerful Christmas trees were banished—never mind Santa and the Baby Jesus.

This airport at the edge of the continent where Cornelia debarked was instead celebrating "an iconic Northwest winter." Cornelia thought this should involve iconic northwest fir trees, but the ubiquitous evergreens were too similar to you-know-what trees. So the trees instead were made of charred bent metal and glittered with chilly white lights. It was apocalyptic, post-Christmas décor to celebrate a new, post-Christmas holiday. Cornelia couldn't stop thinking of Miss Grace's painting of the Satanic Christmas—a combination of icy barrenness and eternal burning.

The similarities between the visionary painting and Cornelia's current environment gave her the shivers as she passed through the airport. It was as if the Grinch had stolen everything and had stitched together the lips of the Whos in Whoville while they slept. So there was no resilient burst of song from the Whos that caused the Grinch's heart to explode in redemptive love. Cornelia paused to glance around her as the Christmas travelers hurried like survivors through a landscape devoid of Christmas.

She was getting closer to her childhood home, and memories were starting to surge through her. There had been nothing warm-and-fuzzy about Cornelia's childhood with her fiercely private grandmother who had refused government commodities and—unlike the shamelessly exhibitionist Miss Grace—had kept her faith to herself. Cornelia's grandmother had become a pregnant widow thanks to the Vietnam War. With only a high school education, she'd cooked in diners and cafeterias and cleaned offices for a living to support her only son, Cornelia's father. Grandmother had spent her later years raising her own organic vegetables and livestock long before it was trendy, while simultaneously, as it would turn out, raising her granddaughter, Cornelia. Cornelia still recalled her Grandma's heavy, cloth-bound book titled *Organic Gardening*. It was always laying around, and well-thumbed. That seemed to be her grandmother's Bible. It struck Cornelia now that Grandma hadn't been in it—religion, that is—for blessings, money or health. She had expected no such frills from God. But she had quietly passed her faith on, praying with Cornelia every night, reading from the Bible, and dutifully taking her to Sunday School. So much of contemporary religion, Cornelia reflected, seemed sadly ramshackle alongside her grandmother's. Today's "believers" seemed so often to have wobbly character, selfish expectations, and a constant demand for divine hand-outs—a ponying-up to collect commodities from God, so to speak.

Cornelia's grandmother often seemed dismissive of Miss Grace's flights of fancy, yet she must have, in her grave and quiet way, believed the Bible—even the Book of Revelation. During the Reagan years, just before Cornelia was born, Grandmother had kept a "nuclear fall-out shelter" well-stocked with canned fruits and vegetables, in case, she said, of national emergency. It was just a dank old root cellar, and in later years Grandma kept it locked up tight out of fear that Cornelia would somehow wind up injured if she descended down the crumbly steps. But Grandma herself had visited it regularly and kept the shelves lined with provisions throughout Cornelia's childhood, even after the Cold War—just in case the end was near.

And so Cornelia came full circle back to the Book of Revelation and its swarming images of the End Times. She came back to the painting. And she had a disquieting thought. Suppose the Satanic holiday had already, at least in some quarters, commenced. What if the chilly airport decor was something like a dress rehearsal—a stripping away of Christmas in preparation for a gift exchange of a more sinister kind?

Then who were the Two Witnesses whose death would be so raucously celebrated? And where were they now?

Cornelia's probing question from childhood had never been answered. She had gone home that night with Grandma, who had read to her from the Book of Revelation, as Miss Grace had admonished she should. That night Cornelia heard the story of the people of the world, plagued by the fiery words of the Two Witnesses. And so the Two Witnesses had been duly slaughtered, their corpses left in the street, while the people celebrated with their foul, new-fangled holiday.

But surely those two witnesses couldn't have already come and gone—breathing fire, tormenting the world, and being slain in the street—without Cornelia noticing?

"Who are the two witnesses?" she'd whispered as a child, tucked beneath a quilt, smiling with concern.

"I'm not sure if I know the answer to that," Grandma had replied patiently. "As you see, God's Word keeps that secret. He reveals it when He wishes."

"Does Miss Grace know who the two witnesses are?" Cornelia asked hopefully. Now that they'd cracked open the door to this mystery, she wanted the full story.

Her grandmother's sudden smile surprised her. "I doubt it. Really, she's just a mystery lover at heart. She loves a good puzzle. That's why she—well, she and I have that in common. I suppose we all get it from our Creator. Sometimes I think God loves strewing the clues. We end up tracking them." Grandma sighed deeply and smoothed her hair. She abruptly plunged into a flight of fancy, which Cornelia had never heard before and would never hear again. "When Miss Grace paints, the Holy Spirit is issuing onto the canvas like a steady stream of fire. Miss Grace's hand has a mind of its own. Or rather, her hand has the Holy Spirit's mind. So even Miss Grace doesn't understand all that she paints. She has ideas about it, though. She has guesses. She knows the answer's in there somewhere. And I expect if you study that painting long enough, you'll find the answers, all right." Grandma paused, and her eyes had a faraway look. "Although she doesn't even consider *Satanic Christmas* to be finished. She believes God still has something else to say about the identity of those Two Witnesses. So, who knows? Perhaps the answer is still on its way."

CHAPTER 5

AMERICAN CHRISTMAS

After twenty-four hours in the air and three plane changes, Cornelia at last touched down in America's heartland. She rented a silver Ford Fusion in the Kansas City airport and then plunged across the border into dark Missouri hills. So she already felt severely disoriented, even before all hell broke loose. She felt intensely nostalgic for the ghosts of Christmas past, and she punched the scan button on the radio hoping to hear old-time Christmas carols. And that's when Miss Grace's voice sucked Cornelia back in time.

The radio was static-filled, as if Miss Grace had catapulted forward from some early radio show just to reach Cornelia. And, in fact, it was *The Old-Time Gospel Hour* that Cornelia had come across on the radio dial. Miss Grace's accent, her nasal twang, even her *words* were a jolt from childhood. Cornelia recalled tossing and turning on hot summer nights beneath the sheets in Grandma's house, while Miss Grace's voice drifted through her window as she strummed the autoharp on her front porch and sang these very words.

For in addition to being a visionary folk artist, Miss Grace had been on local radio all those years ago as a lady preacher, and an autoharp-plucking, hymn-crooner.

And now Miss Grace's words were crackling from Cornelia's car radio.

"Hundred-pound hailstones fall from the sky," Miss Grace sang. "Sing the Scriptures, Sing the Book." She plucked on her autoharp and the hair on the back of Cornelia's neck stood on end.

Decades earlier, when Miss Grace first sang this song, out-of-control weather had seemed like some fantastic sci-fi future. It no longer did. All around Cornelia, she saw the tall, dark trees of her Missouri childhood had been snapped in half, one after the other. The weight of an unbearable ice storm had broken their spines. Then hail had splintered the surviving trunks and tornadoes had uprooted them. Finally, floods had carried the debris away. Cornelia had read on the internet about the seemingly unending string of catastrophes that had struck her childhood home, one after another. But to see the carnage strewn all around her in this icy night was still shocking. The skeletal remains of thousands of trees were now dusted with snow, glowing like a valley of scattered bones.

"Hundred-pound hailstones fall from the sky," Miss Grace sang loudly and nasally. Her voice softened as she continued wonderingly. "But still they did not repent. The people *cursed God* and did not repent."

That part of the Book of Revelation had particularly haunted Cornelia as a child. If 100-pound hailstones are plummeting from the sky, how could anyone curse God and refuse to repent? Wouldn't you rush to repent, praying desperately to survive those terrible hailstones?

"Here at Christmas time, it's good to reflect on how we want God to be Santa Clause," Miss Grace preached. Her voice sounded even more frail and tremulous than Cornelia remembered. "Like spoiled children we are slow to thank God, but quick to blame him."

Cornelia thought again of the stripped-down, sterile airport. Even a *hint* of Christmas, like the evergreen tree, had been expunged from the busy terminal. She thought, in contrast, of how proud and unapologetic Thailand was of its rich Buddhist heritage, and how exuberantly it celebrated its many Buddhist holidays.

"Have you noticed the fear in our country these days?" Miss Grace asked, her voice trembling. "Why are we so afraid these days of the roaring of the seas, of signs in the sun and the moon and the stars?"

Miss Grace's theory: It was the End Times.

"We fear because we know the truth deep down. Our country has been full of our good Lord's Christmas gifts. But do we give Him credit? No, we do not! We say: Look at what *we've* amassed! And secretly, we plot to evict our Creator lest he interfere too much in our lucky lives." Miss Grace paused here to strum mournfully on her autoharp. "We send our dear Lord out into the lonely night with a smile. We celebrate our newfound freedom and pretend he never existed. But there's a new knock at the door!" Miss Grace stopped strumming and sharply clapped her hands. She let the airwaves crackle, just a beat too long, in dead silence. For a moment Cornelia thought the signal had been lost. When Miss Grace continued, her voice was almost a whisper. "There's a wolf at the door. But we have sent our *Savior* away. So who will save us now?" Miss Grace strummed. "Merry Christmas!"

Cornelia laughed out loud. Miss Grace's unvarnished prophecy of doom was coupled with cheery Christmas greetings. *Merry Christmas.* And her voice had been sincere, not sarcastic. Then Cornelia's smile faded. Cornelia had boxed up her memories of Miss Grace—along with numerous other memories—and put them on the shelf like forgotten photographs. But the weight of that out-of-place painting had brought the shelf tumbling down. All those memories of Grandma's words, of Miss Grace's words, about "our dear Lord" had spilled out. And the simple truth was that the painting worried Cornelia far more now than it had as a child. As a child, she'd been fascinated and curious. Now she felt uneasy. Was it because they were eighteen years closer to the events depicted? The painting seemed to portend some grim, grim Christmas which wasn't very far away. Or was Cornelia worried about that painting because it felt like the painting had found her and was trying to tell her something?

Another part of Cornelia was worried about herself. She had spent the last five years of her life completely cut off from her past, immersed in the bubbling misery of a massive Asian slum. Maybe, just maybe, she had lost touch with reality. That happened, Cornelia had noticed, to ex-pats who stayed away from home too long. They couldn't fit in anymore. And sometimes, because they were no longer moored to a home and a history, they simply went round the bend, never to return. They spent the rest of their lives as odd drifters with no real connection anywhere. They no longer knew how to relate in a deep and lasting way—only in that superficial, passing way in which travelers briefly bond. Cornelia had encountered eccentric ex-pats during her time overseas—they were like ghosts of who they had formerly been.

Maybe *that's* why Cornelia was reacting—overreacting?—to *Satanic Christmas.* Maybe the painting's magnetic pull was a sign that she herself had become one of those spirits adrift—that some last shred of her former self was clinging to the painting-from-her-past like a life preserver.

With *The Old-Time Gospel Hour* ended, the radio was now playing a money management program based on sound scriptural principles. Cornelia turned down the volume so that all she heard was the rhythmic beating of the windshield wipers. Scattered snowflakes melted instantly on the windshield, and headlights from oncoming cars flared brightly in the night before disappearing.

And then the strangest thought flickered in Cornelia's mind— what if Miss Grace herself were one of the Two Witnesses? On the surface, it seemed ludicrous—but Miss Grace was nothing if not a witness. What if Miss Grace's sermons, her paintings, her songs—all emitting from an unlikely little lady in an obscure spot on the map—were chock full of dire warnings and urgent pleas to an unbelieving world? *What exactly had the Two Witnesses said that so enraged the madding crowd?* Cornelia would have to crack open a Bible again, for the first time in many years.

As she drove, an image of young children dying of AIDS in the slum flashed through her mind. She saw their skeletal frames curled pitifully in their beds. Yes, they had been in peril. And a part of Cornelia had thought at first that she could rescue them. But she hadn't. Others had, by bringing in the medicine that would prolong their lives. All Cornelia had done was visit, hold their hands, teach them, for no good reason, the ABCs.

So now, if something were unfolding on a cosmic level, what made Cornelia think *she* could make a difference? Yet she couldn't shake a crazy feeling that finding the painting in Bangkok had been a *summons*. Was Miss Grace herself in danger? Was she one of the Two Witnesses? And if Miss Grace were one of the Two Witnesses—*who was the other one?* Cornelia held out a lonely hope as she drove toward Newton, Missouri that cold, dark night just before Christmas, with the empty anti-Christmas décor of the airport still glittering coldly in her mind. Miss Grace obviously thought this country was in trouble. *A wolf is at the door.* Was she right, or just a crazy old lady? Whichever it was, Cornelia felt somewhat comforted that there were still Miss Graces around, hidden in the remote dark hills of America, seeding the landscape with solemn songs and pure prayers on late-night radio.

CHAPTER 6
MISS GRACE

Cornelia was amazed. She parked her car on the quiet Main Street of Newton, Missouri and stared. Only one other car was parked on the street, but Ted's Barber Shop was still standing. Next to the barber shop lay the weedy ruins of the abandoned gas pumps. The only other building was Wrigley's General Store, a plain wooden structure painted white and trimmed in green. Cornelia could see lights on inside.

When she pushed the heavy door open, a bell tinkled, just as she remembered. She was instantly submerged in childhood memories—the sloping wooden floor which left her feeling slightly off-balance, the burnished bronze-and-glass post office boxes where she picked up Grandma's mail every day. She had always headed for the candy section—a popsicle in summer, a sugar-filled Dixie straw in winter. At the far end of the store was a soda fountain counter, where a customer sat on a red stool, elbows propped on the white Formica. Behind the counter, a man wearing a grease-stained apron was re-filling the customer's coffee cup.

"Can I help you?" the man called. He had thick silver hair and a chiseled jaw, like a movie star from an earlier generation. "I'm getting ready to close up."

That's when Cornelia's cell phone rang. It was Chanya.

"I'm *here*," she said, hardly able to contain her excitement. "I'm in Wrigley's Store. It's *exactly* the same. I'm about to go see Miss Grace. I'm going to tell her I found *Satanic Christmas* and ask her about the missing twin."

Chanya sounded distant, but maybe it was the connection. "What missing twin? And when do you think you'll come back?"

"It depends on how things go here. Chanya, it's *Christmas* time here, and there's snow on the ground, and Ted's Barber Shop is still here, and it's still decorated with red-and-green lights and that big star on top! I used to go *caroling* there and he'd give us candy!"

"What? Who's Ted?" Chanya sounded agitated.

"Listen," Cornelia said. "I really have to go. It's getting pretty late here, and I don't know how early Miss Grace goes to bed. I'll call you with an update as soon as I can." As she hung up, she felt slightly disappointed that Chanya didn't seem to be sharing her enthusiasm for re-discovering her roots. But there were a lot of miles between them.

"Did you need something?" the Cary Grant look-alike behind the counter called again. He was watching Cornelia intently.

"No, it's O.K.," Cornelia replied. "I just wanted to see the store again."

"I should probably tell you," he said. "I overheard your phone conversation. If you're here to see Miss Grace, I'm afraid you're too late."

⇒⊹ ⊹⇐

The woman standing in the doorway of Miss Grace's house blinked at Cornelia tiredly. She had brown hair streaked with gray and wore light blue sweats. Her cheeks were flushed, as if she'd been exercising. In the background, Cornelia could hear someone shouting commands on a television to squat deeper.

"Miss Grace passed away about a year ago," the woman said. "Are you here about the paintings?"

"Yes," Cornelia said, her hope rising. "I am."

The woman glared. "Well, I have nothing to say about that. I'm sorry."

Cornelia braced herself. She was exhausted. She had jet lag and she couldn't believe she'd come all this way to see Miss Grace, too late. She smiled.

"I just flew in from Thailand. I—"

"Look. We don't have anything to do with her paintings anymore. If you're interested in collecting them, I'd recommend E-bay. I'm sorry you came all this way for nothing."

"No, you don't understand," Cornelia said calmly. "I used to live right there—" Cornelia pointed across the street. "I grew up across the street from Miss Grace. My grandmother died five years ago and I've been living overseas ever since. I just flew in. I'd really hoped to see Miss Grace. Could you—could you at least point me to her grave?" At the very least, Cornelia could pay her respects.

The woman's eyes widened.

"I remember you! You were just a little girl when I used to visit. Aunt Grace used to call you Smiling Cornelia. She said you were quiet, but you never stopped smiling."

Cornelia nodded. "Cornelia Small. And I'm not just here about the paintings. It's also about my grandmother, and home—" She gestured weakly across the street. "And—everything. I came back to see what was left."

"Yes!" the woman agreed, sounding excited. "I'm Marcella, Miss Grace's niece. I think you'd better come in."

⚔ ⚔

Cornelia dunked her bag of decaffeinated Earl Grey up and down in her tea cup. She was sitting in a red, overstuffed chair

next to a cold fireplace. On each arm of the chair was a delicate faded doily. Cornelia touched the yellowed lace, certain that
she had fingered the same doilies as a child, except then they'd
been crisp and white. Miss Grace was gone, and Cornelia didn't
know what she was doing in what was now Marcella's living room.
How could Miss Grace's niece help? Cornelia seized the warm
tea cup with both hands and tried to steady herself. The cup and
saucer were made of delicate white china decorated with pink
roses. Cornelia remembered these, too. In one corner of the
living room, a Scotch pine Christmas tree glittered with multi-
colored lights. A rather gaudy blinking star flashed from the top
of the tree. A handful of wrapped gifts were beneath the tree.
The sharp fragrance of the tree absolutely made Cornelia feel
like it was Christmas time, and she was really home. She looked
up from her cup at Marcella.

Marcella beamed. "You *still* have a disarming smile."

"Do I?" Cornelia asked, surprised. She hadn't even realized she
was smiling.

Marcella cocked her head, openly studying Cornelia. "Otherwise
you'd have a severe expression because of those dark eyebrows."
She paused. "You got your eyebrows from your grandmother."

Embarrassed, Cornelia took a sip of tea, which was sweet
from sugar. The only sound in the room was the ticking of the
wall clock—a china plate with the same pink rose pattern, along
with black clock hands and delicately painted black numbers. Miss
Grace's furnishings still occupied much of the room, although a
large Curtis Mathes console TV squatted in the middle of the room
encased in a wood veneer cabinet. On top of it perched a newer,
smaller Sony Trinitron which was now muted, a thin young woman
on screen leading exercises, her mouth moving silently. Cornelia
was certain that neither television had belonged to Miss Grace. In
fact, Miss Grace's fame as a gospel performer had begun in childhood in the church, and spread via radio. Cornelia remembered a

polished walnut RCA Victor radio almost as tall as she was standing in the same place where the televisions were now.

"Those paintings," Marcella sighed, hunching over and looking down into her own steaming cup. "They have been the bane of our existence. Still are! You're the second person today to ask me about them."

"The second person today?" Cornelia tried to hide her surprise.

"A man knocked on the door earlier, wanting to buy them. He said his name was Vic, Victor, something like that. I told him there was nothing left to buy from me. He seemed none too pleased. Believe me, we wanted nothing more than to be rid of those two paintings." She glanced up at Cornelia quickly. "No offense. It's just that we were—I can only use the word *harassed*—after Aunt Grace died. Collectors, dealers, art critics, *reporters*." Marcella spat the last word out. "They all wanted a look at those last two pieces. The two "lost paintings," they called them. Well, they were the only two paintings she never sold. They were never *lost*."

"No," Cornelia agreed slowly. "I remember *Satanic Christmas*. As a little girl."

"Why sure you did!" Marcella exclaimed, sounding excited again. "If anyone would have seen those so-called "lost paintings," it would be you."

Cornelia's gaze wandered to the mantle above the fireplace which was draped with fake green Christmas tinsel and crowded with family photographs. In one photograph, Miss Grace stood petite and beaming in a pink-and-white checkered gingham dress with puffy sleeves and skirt. Her fine white hair hovered like a cloud above her head, her big blue eyes child-like and sparkling. In sharp contrast, Cornelia's grandmother stood tall and unsmiling beside Miss Grace, her own white hair pulled into a tight bun, her pale blue dress plain except for a narrow black belt at the waist. Cornelia was sandwiched between the two women, her smile shy, her ponytailed hair almost as white as the women on either side of her. Marcella was right. Both Cornelia and her grandmother shared the same straight black eyebrows, although on her grandmother they were forbidding. Softened by Cornelia's smile and youth, her eyebrows were simply striking.

"Yes, I did see her paintings a lot," Cornelia agreed. "We visited your aunt every day."

Marcella gave Cornelia a peculiar glance. "Well, we knew we had to keep them for you." She looked searchingly at Cornelia, her expression suddenly warm. "But we had no idea where you were. It seems like a miracle that you're here. Just showing up on my doorstep. And—" Marcella looked uncomfortable. "I can only apologize on behalf of my brother, Frank. He had no business selling *Satanic Christmas*. None. It was not ours to sell. That priest wanted it so badly, though. And Frank said you were never coming back. He said we could give you the money for it if you ever showed up." Marcella looked earnestly at Cornelia. "I wasn't around when it happened. I would never have allowed Frank to do that. And I *will* give you the money for it. I've been using a little each month to pay for the storage locker. But that's all I've spent of the money." She looked guiltily at Cornelia, as if waiting for absolution.

Cornelia had been listening as patiently as she knew how, trying to fit the pieces together in her mind as Marcella talked. Something wasn't right.

"But it *was* yours to sell," she said slowly. "Why were you saving the paintings for me?"

"Well, they were yours," Marcella said, sounding surprised.

"You mean your Aunt Grace left them to *me*?" Cornelia asked. "But why me?"

"Your grandmother had just left the paintings with Aunt Grace for safekeeping. She never meant for Aunt Grace to keep them permanently."

Cornelia was completely confused now.

"You mean Miss Grace gave the paintings to my grandmother as gifts?" Cornelia had a dizzying image of Miss Grace and her grandmother toting the paintings back and forth across the street, taking turns giving them to each other. Marcella was looking at Cornelia with something like dawning horror.

"You don't know," she said numbly.

"I don't know what?" Cornelia asked, apprehensively.

"Of course you don't know. Who would have told you? I thought maybe, somehow, she'd told you after all." Marcella sighed. "Your grandmother was the artist. She painted *Satanic Christmas*. And its twin, *Apocalypse*. She painted them all."

Cornelia nearly dropped her cup. Tea slopped over the cup rim. It took her a moment to find her voice. "That's ridiculous," she said weakly.

"No," Marcella said, an edge in her voice. "If only your grandmother had not insisted on anonymity. Her early paintings were unsigned. But after they started attracting the attention of the art world, after people started asking questions about the artist, Aunt Grace agreed to pretend to be the painter. It has caused us a lot of unnecessary grief. A lot of *embarrassment*."

"But I would have *noticed* if my grandmother had been painting all day," Cornelia objected.

"You were at school all day," Marcella pointed out. "How old were you when you moved in with your grandmother?"

"Ten," Cornelia said. "Yes, I was going to school every day. But I would have noticed the paints, the canvasses, the mess."

Marcella shrugged. "Your grandmother painted in the root cellar. Right after she died, Aunt Grace went down there and cleaned out all the supplies. Lamps, magnifying glasses, sketch pads, paints. She was very protective of your grandmother's secret. Your grandmother had told her to never sell two paintings—*Apocalypse* and *Satanic Christmas*—that it was imperative they be passed on to you. She said they were twins. She said *Satanic Christmas* revealed the true identity of the Two Witnesses. And *Apocalypse* revealed their true message." Marcella snorted. "I personally never understood what all the fuss was about. Those paintings were just—*crazy*. I never saw any message in them. Nothing you couldn't already read in the Bible, anyway. Everyone knows who the Two Witnesses are. Half of the paintings were just Bible verses re-written. How hard is that to paint?" She glanced apologetically at Cornelia. "I mean, no offense to your grandmother. I'm sure she had a talent. The attention just seemed to me...overblown."

Marcella kept talking, but Cornelia was in shock. The locked root cellar of her childhood. The one her grandmother warned could only bring accidents and harm. Cornelia recalled being in there once, on a stormy night during a tornado warning. They had sat on the cellar steps with a flashlight and a radio and never even descended into the inky depths. Cornelia saw the occasional gleam of canned beets and tomatoes lining the shelves. She smelled the musty earth below, and imagined the spiders. She hated spiders, and that fear alone kept her out of the root cellar. Cornelia had a vague memory of tarps in the cellar, tarps covering—what? Tables covered with dusty bell jars? Canning equipment that had fallen into disuse? Just a root cellar's clutter, she'd thought at the time. Now she realized those tarps were probably covering the paintings and art supplies.

Cornelia had also gone down into the cellar after her grandmother died, just before she sold the house. Cornelia was teaching English at a small college near Kansas City at the time, and had returned to Newton to settle her grandmother's affairs. But as Marcella said, the concrete cellar floor was empty and swept clean. The shelves were rotting and bare. She was amazed that it had frightened her so as a child. It *had* held one surprise, though. At the bottom of the stairs was a light switch. When Cornelia flicked it on, the cellar was flooded with light. In her childhood, she'd assumed the cellar had no lighting at all, or at best a dim, flickering bulb with an unreliable yank chain. During the day, if her grandmother ventured there to retrieve canned goods, daylight filtered down weakly from the raised cellar door. Cornelia might see Grandmother below in the semi-darkness, moving amongst the tarp-covered tables, reaching for jars of pickles or peaches. If Grandmother and Cornelia were forced into the cellar on a stormy night, they always waited on the top steps with a flashlight until the storm subsided. The cellar steps were deadly for a young girl. The cellar depths were strictly off-limits.

"Why did my grandmother hide her identity?" Cornelia asked. But she already knew the answer. Her grandmother was a fiercely private woman. She had gone through the school of hard knocks early in life, and she had a general distrust of people. On the other hand, Miss Grace had been an exhibitionist, a performer. She thrived in the limelight. She had been in the public eye singing and preaching since she was a child. She was revered and respected in her church world. Miss Grace wasn't just a nattering old fool whom Grandma had tolerated, Cornelia now realized. Miss Grace had been in on the scheme. Grandma had *trusted* her.

"Your grandmother thought she had a responsibility to share the messages she received in her paintings, but she didn't want the attention," Marcella said. "Aunt Grace posed as the artist, even signed the paintings and sold them. But she passed the checks back to your grandmother." Marcella hesitated. "Your grandmother told Aunt Grace that she only wanted some of the sales money for you, for your future. Your grandmother offered my aunt a "commission" every time she sold a painting. But Aunt Grace refused to take a commission, to take anything. This has always made Frank bitter."

Cornelia's mind reeled. Her inheritance explained. She had always wondered how it could have come from selling organic eggs. "Why didn't Miss Grace tell *me* all of this?" she wondered aloud.

"Aunt Grace only told me on her deathbed, as she was dying," Marcella replied. "You weren't around and no one knew how to contact you. You had disappeared right after your grandmother died. I think Aunt Grace always assumed you would come back home again and she would have a chance to tell you everything. She hadn't counted on you going away for good. It's hard for the old people to adjust to the world we live in today. All our roots severed, our families scattered. All of us adrift."

Marcella's voice wasn't accusing, but Cornelia felt a stab of guilt anyway. Marcella had pegged her right. Cornelia lifted the cup of tea to her lips and noticed it was cold.

"You know, Aunt Grace drove all the reporters crazy," Marcella said sadly. "She gave evasive non-answers. She would preach and prattle on. But how could she answer all their probing questions about her paintings? *She wasn't the artist.*" She gave Cornelia an aggressive stare. "It wasn't fair to her. And it wasn't fair to us."

"Because of how they hounded you once she'd died?" Cornelia asked guiltily.

"Yes, and all the attention we received. Some of it negative. They even started writing articles about the rest of her family, about *us.*"

Marcella's lip quivered, and Cornelia was horrified to see she was about to cry. "The way they presented us, as backwoods hicks and rubes. This part of the country as ignorant and stupid. And Aunt Grace as mentally ill. But none of them minded cashing in on those paintings." She picked up her tea cup and Cornelia noticed her hand shook. "Pardon my outburst."

"I'm *sorry,*" Cornelia said fervently. She felt angry on behalf of poor Marcella and Frank. "I didn't know."

Marcella wiped her eyes and gave Cornelia a defeated smile. "I know. You were just a little girl. Your grandmother was protecting herself and you, but it turned out to be at our family's expense. She knew Aunt Grace was all alone, with no husband or children, and she knew Aunt Grace's temperament, that she would just float serenely above the fray. It must have seemed like the perfect solution. Your grandmother assumed, wrongly, that no one could be harmed by it." Unburdened, Marcella shoved a lock of hair out of her eyes and smiled tepidly. "Anyway, the last painting is yours. After Aunt Grace died, this house was broken into twice, and after that I moved the painting to a storage locker in Joplin. It's climate-controlled," she hastened to add. "The painting is crated up, protected. I know it's late now, but I can meet you there tomorrow morning, first thing, and give you the painting. Nine a.m.? And I'll bring the money we owe you."

"No money," Cornelia said quickly. She was feeling more than a little guilty about the burden Marcella had been bearing in her stead. "Just keep the money. For all your help and trouble." Cornelia touched the silver locket from her grandmother which she wore perpetually round her neck. Inside the locket was a miniature pen-and-ink portrait of Cornelia's father. Grandmother had always said that Miss Grace was the artist. Now Cornelia realized it was probably drawn by Grandmother herself. Marcella had seen magnifying glasses in Grandmother's art supplies, the better to see with when drawing in miniature. Beneath the locket, Cornelia felt her pulse jump in her throat. "Please tell me one last thing. You said everyone knows who the Two Witnesses are." Cornelia suddenly felt embarrassed about her ignorance. "Well, I don't. Who are they?"

"Moses and Elijah returned from the dead," Marcella said firmly. "They'll walk around in our modern world, appearing on TV, in their robes and white beards. People will get fed up and kill them. Moses represents the Law, you know. And Elijah represents the Prophets. Moses lays down the rules, and Elijah warns against breaking them."

No, Cornelia didn't know. She didn't know any of that. Her Sunday School learning was far rustier than she'd realized. "And that's in the Book of Revelation?" she asked, wracking her brain for a recollection of this part of the story. Two old guys walking around in their white beards and robes on T.V.?

"Well," Marcella hesitated. "I'm not sure if it's *explicitly* in the Book of Revelation. Maybe you have to read between the lines. Some people say the Two Witnesses are Elijah and Enoch, because they were sucked up into the sky. Never died. That's how they can come back, still alive." Marcella shrugged. "It's two old men from the Old Testament. I'm not sure which. But the answer's in there, all right."

Just what Grandma said about the paintings, it occurred to Cornelia as she stepped out into the dark night. *The answer is in the paintings.* The street was completely silent except for a distant barking dog. This was exactly her recollection of nighttime in Newton. It couldn't have been a sharper contrast to the non-stop noise and light of Bangkok. Marcella had switched off her outdoor Christmas lights, and Cornelia craned her neck and looked up at the cold sky, glittering with stars. She slid behind the wheel of the rental car, wishing she had gloves, and glanced down at her cellphone. No messages. No calls. No Chanya. Her cellphone wallpaper rotated regularly through images stored on her phone, and at this moment she was treated to a photo of herself standing in front of Wat Arun on the banks of the Chao Praya River. The ancient spires of the Temple of Dawn soared in the background, dwarfing Cornelia, while in the foreground, water taxis glided back and forth on the river. The tropical sun was bright, the water blue, and Cornelia was smiling. Here in the dark and cold of tiny Newton, Missouri, that person on her phone screen seemed a million miles away, in another life. Cornelia shivered, since all she'd brought with her from Thailand was her red athletic jacket. As she turned on the ignition, the heater blasting cold air, she heard another car start up just across the street. Its headlights sprang to life, the driver also pulling away from the curb. The driver is a smoker, Cornelia thought tiredly as she rolled out of town and back toward the highway. Briefly, she saw the orange glow of a cigarette inside the dark car.

CHAPTER 7

APOCALYPSE

The next morning, Cornelia sat in *The Colonel's Pancake House* in Joplin with a feeling of foreboding. Jetlagged as she'd been, she should have slept like a rock the night before. But she kept waking up in the midst of a turbulent dream. In an endless and confused narrative, Miss Grace and Grandma were the Two Witnesses. They kept showing up on her doorstep—sometimes at Grandma's house in Newton, sometimes in Cornelia's little studio apartment on the slum's edge in Bangkok, dressed exactly as they were in the photograph on Marcella's mantle, in frilly pink ging-ham and no-nonsense blue. And they would begin to talk. And talk. But this was the catch—no sound came out of their mouths. The volume was turned off. The Two Witnesses were mute. They were trying desperately to impart a message to Cornelia. And she was trying with all her might to read their lips, to catch an audible syllable from their furiously-moving mouths. But she couldn't un-derstand a word they were saying.

So she was relieved to awake to winter sun streaming through the blinds of her motel room. She showered and stopped at the pancake house in Joplin. She and her grandmother had eaten here on numerous occasions when she was young, sometimes after church on Sunday. She remembered the first time they ate there. It was not long after her parents' funeral, after the car accident, and it had just been decided that she would now live with her grandmother. Her anti-social grandmother must have been overwhelmed by all that was happening in both their lives, for she had invited her entire Sunday School class to join them—the first and only time she ever did this. The ladies sipped coffee and chattered and patted Cornelia frequently on the head and hand. They promised to introduce her to their grandchildren and harangued her grandmother about signing her up for Sunday School immediately. One of the women was quiet and serious and watched Cornelia somberly the entire time. She had dyed black hair, bright red lipstick and sparkly cat glasses, which Cornelia had never forgotten. As they departed from the restaurant, the woman murmured to her grandmother. "Just you remember, Elizabeth. The Lord looks after the widows and the orphans."

The brutality of the word shocked Cornelia. *Orphan.* She knew then that the first part of her young life was decisively over. Something irrevocable had happened to her and her new life had just begun: She was now and would forever be *an orphan.*

That was when Cornelia was ten years old, but the memory still sent a shudder through her. She had definitely stirred up old ghosts by returning home. It made her think of one of the young girls she taught in the slum, Kanjana. Kanjana's father had dropped her off at the emergency room because she couldn't breathe. Kanjana was in need of a repaired heart, which she miraculously received, at the hands of skilled doctors, in the nick of time. But her father never picked her up again. Cornelia still recalled the exact, anguished moment in the hospital ward when Kanjana understood her father wasn't ever going to take her home again. Home was a one-room shack with two little sisters, and a father who was hopelessly addicted to drugs. But still, it was home. It was the only world Kanjana had ever known. And now she knew it was gone. Her father was overwhelmed by responsibility he was not living up to. It was easier to just let Kanjana go. Kanjana could imagine no other future, of course—once her father, her only anchor, cut her loose, where in the world would she float to?

As Cornelia dug around in her purse for a tip, it occurred to her that someone was watching her. She felt eyes boring into her back and turned around. It was a man, with thinning brown hair and a bristly, unshaven face. He instantly looked down and picked up his coffee cup, thrusting it to his lips.

Steeped as Cornelia was in memories, she had a crazy thought. Could he be someone who recognized her from her childhood? Or was he just a pancake-house regular who knew she was a stranger? Just then, her cell phone rang. It was Chanya.

She filled him in on as much as she could of her conversation with Marcella the night before.

"I can't talk now, though. I'm going to meet Marcella right now at the—" She peered at her note. "*U-Store-It* Storage Lockers. To pick up the twin painting! I can't wait to get the two paintings side by side and try to figure this whole thing out."

"When are you coming back?" Chanya asked. Was Cornelia imagining it, or was there genuine longing in his voice as he spoke to her? He was saying something else, about the dinner planned in his honor, but the connection was fading.

"I'll be there soon," Cornelia promised again, just before their connection died completely. On her cell phone screen, the image of Miss Grace, Grandmother, and ten-year-old Cornelia swam into focus. Cornelia had snapped the photo after asking permission from Marcella the night before. Marcella had tried to give the framed photograph to Cornelia, but Cornelia waved her away, insisting Marcella return the photograph to its spot on the fireplace mantle.

"A real photograph is just something else to travel with," Cornelia explained. "This is better."

The image floating into view on her cellphone screen was an eerie reminder of her unsettling *Two Witnesses* dream from the night before. There they were again, in pink gingham and plain blue, trying to speak to Cornelia, yet helpless and mute.

Cornelia stood. It was past nine o'clock. She was already late meeting Marcella at the storage locker. The man at the nearby table had gone. She dropped the change on the table and left.

It took Cornelia a while to find it. It was in a new part of Joplin she'd never been to before. That there were "new parts" of Joplin still surprised Cornelia. Before the tornado, Joplin had appeared suspended in time to Cornelia, and she had selfishly and nostalgically wanted it to stay that way. It had grown up from small town to small city thanks to Route 66—Cornelia herself had been born in a hospital just off the busy crossroads of America. All along the highways that coursed like veins through Joplin's heart had been neon reminders of the past—motels, diners, drive-in restaurants. One of Cornelia's most vivid memories of her grandmother was when she spoke eagerly about growing up in the hubbub of downtown Joplin with its glitzy Fox Theater and crowded city buses and glamorous department stores which offered unimaginable luxuries such as escalators and elevators.

"Those were the days," her grandmother had often said wistfully. "Things started to change as I was growing up. The whole country was changing. Then I met your grandfather at that drag race on the edge of town. My mother did not approve of him, not one bit."

When Cornelia's grandfather left for Vietnam in 1965, he left behind a pregnant, twenty-two-year-old wife. He was a helicopter pilot who was busy rescuing wounded soldiers under enemy fire when his CH-46A transport helicopter took several direct hits and spiraled down into the jungle. His body was never recovered. In many ways, Cornelia's grandmother never recovered, either.

Since that time, Joplin had been changing along with the rest of the country and had its own new developments and sprawl, even before the tornado which had brutally wiped clean the heart of the town. Despite the leafy old trees which shaded the rest of Joplin, there were no trees in the tornado zone, and all construction was brand new. *U-Store-It* was a shiny new facility on the west edge of town where new growth was occurring. As Cornelia pulled in to the storage facility, a maroon sedan roared past her on its way out. Other than that, she saw no sign of life as she drove slowly through the alleyways lined with storage lockers and patches of dirty snow. Marcella had told her to meet at Number 112, and since Cornelia was running late, she expected Marcella to be waiting for her. Cornelia recognized Marcella's car, a white Ford Escort turned gray by winter's grime. But the garage door to 112 was still shut and padlocked. Cornelia stepped out of the car into a biting breeze and looked around. It was sunny but freezing. Cornelia saw no one else in sight. She walked over to the garage door and rattled the handle. And that's when Cornelia heard her. First she heard shouting, and then pounding on the door.

"I'm inside!" Marcella cried. "He locked me in!"

"Marcella?" Cornelia called. "You're locked inside?" She rattled the locked door once more. "Where's the key?"

"He took it," Marcella shouted. "Try the office manager. He'll have to cut the padlock so you can get in. Hurry up! It's freezing in here!"

It probably would have been faster to drive to the office, but Cornelia was so shocked by this turn of events that she turned and started running. She had always been a runner. She'd been light as a feather as a child, and after being discovered by a coach on the grade school playground, instantly became a star on the track team. When she ran like the wind with her ponytail streaming behind, it was like she'd entered into another dimension, and everyone commented that she never stopped smiling even when she ran. Even as an adult, Cornelia still ran for exercise—but she felt like she was slowing down as she grew older, as if she'd finally outraced the pain of her past, and had arrived, safe and sound, in the present.

Cornelia sprinted the remaining distance to the office. Thankfully, a bald older man wearing wire-frame glasses was sitting at his computer when Cornelia burst in. After a few moments of initial confusion, the short, wiry man hauled himself out of his creaky chair and pulled on a tan sheepskin coat in response to Cornelia's urgency.

"She's locked in, you'll have to cut the lock," Cornelia said, trying to catch her breath.

"Got bolt cutters, hold on a sec," the manager said, fumbling around in a tool box concealed behind his metal desk. Bolt cutters in hand, he jumped on an electric cart parked outside the office, which Cornelia hopped on as well. They sped back to Storage Unit 112, where he proceeded to destroy the padlock and set Marcella free. The office manager was perplexed, Marcella was distraught, and Cornelia felt sick about what she already knew had happened.

"Someone *put* you in there?" the office manager asked. "Why?"

"He demanded the painting," Marcella said. She turned a stricken look on Cornelia. "He took *Apocalypse*. And then he locked me inside. He had a gun," she added, almost as an afterthought.

"He had a *gun?*" the office manager repeated, shocked. "You mean he robbed you? Right here in broad daylight?"

"Yes," Marcella said. "He robbed me. It was—" she turned to Cornelia, distressed. "It was the man who wanted to buy paintings yesterday, before you arrived. His name was Vic. Or so he said." Marcella sounded mystified. "I definitely told him we didn't have any more paintings. I *never* told him we still had the twin."

"I think I saw his car," Cornelia said sadly, recalling the maroon car that had raced past her as she drove in.

"I've had people try to break into the storage lockers at night before," the office manager said. "But no customer has ever been robbed at gunpoint in broad daylight. He must be a meth addict. The meth labs have sprouted up like poisonous mushrooms around here. They're rotting this country's soul."

⊱ ⊰

The morning had been a complete disaster, but not a complete loss. The first good thing that emerged from the disastrous morning was the police artist's sketch of "Vic," based on Marcella's description. A police detective made a copy for Cornelia to take with her.

"I saw Vic in the Colonel's Pancake House this morning," Cornelia said, after looking at the likeness. "In fact, I think he was drinking coffee at Wrigley's Store last night, though I didn't really see his face then—just his back. It must have been after he left your house, Marcella. After you told him you didn't have any paintings."

Marcella looked troubled. "I wonder..."

"I do, too," Cornelia said. "Maybe Vic just wanted a cup of coffee before he hit the road. Or maybe he wasn't satisfied with your answer. Maybe he was even hoping to break in later, when you were asleep, to look around."

Marcella shuddered. "There was something in his demeanor that bothered me. He wasn't a bit happy when I told him I had no more paintings. And my husband is on the road right now. I would have been alone."

Cornelia nodded sympathetically. "Whatever the reason for Vic being at Wrigley's Store, he must have heard my phone conversation with Chanya. I know the store owner overheard me, because he told me I was too late, that Miss Grace had already passed. So Vic heard I was looking for Miss Grace and the missing twin painting." Cornelia remembered the only other car parked on Newton's Main Street, a cigarette smoker behind the wheel. "And he followed me. To my motel last night. To the Colonel's Pancake House this morning." She winced. "This morning, I told Chanya where the painting was being stored. Vic was listening."

"Why would someone be after this painting?" the detective asked Marcella and Cornelia. The two women exchanged uneasy glances.

"It's somewhat valuable," Marcella said grudgingly. "People in the art world are interested in it. We've had people break into our house before, which was why we moved it to a storage locker in the first place."

Cornelia was thoughtful. It seemed that a good many people were avidly interested in both paintings. Interested parties seemed, in fact, to be coming out of the woodwork, in both Bangkok and Missouri. Could Vic be the same man who had sold the painting to the Thai clerk, before heading to the States in search of the missing twin painting? Or was this armed robber just some lunatic obsessed with either apocalyptic art or the money to be made from it? Unfortunately, she had neither a name nor a description of the man who sold *Satanic Christmas* to *The Secret Value Shop* in Bangkok.

The second curious development of the morning occurred as they were leaving the police station, and Marcella pulled Cornelia aside.

"Listen," she said. "I remembered after we talked last night that Aunt Grace had written you a letter. She asked me to give it to you. I found it last night and brought it with me. At least he didn't get that."

"A letter?" Cornelia took the letter from Marcella's outstretched hand. "About what?"

Marcella flashed a wry smile. "I don't know. I don't read other people's personal correspondence. I know Aunt Grace thought the world of your grandmother and felt very protective toward you. Maybe it's along those lines. A goodbye, I'd guess." Marcella shrugged. "Aunt Grace felt bad she had missed her chance to tell you the truth about your grandmother's paintings. Maybe an apology, as well."

Cornelia felt awkward about reading a personal note from Miss Grace in front of Marcella, when Marcella had been excluded from the message and from the paintings' profits. It seemed like rubbing salt in the wound, after Marcella had shouldered the thankless task of watching over the paintings since Miss Grace's death. Cornelia discreetly tucked the envelope in her purse to read in private later. She still had to check out of her motel and return the rental car to the Kansas City airport before catching her flight back to Thailand. She was suffering from a time crunch and also felt sick about losing the painting.

But one final twist came out of that morning, after Cornelia had the presence of mind to ask Marcella a question before they parted.

"You said a priest bought *Satanic Christmas.* Do you know who he was?"

"I don't know his name. But he wore a collar and he told Frank he was a missionary priest on home leave. He had read about Aunt Grace's death and her last two unseen paintings. He said he had an interest in procuring religious art."

"A missionary priest," Cornelia repeated. "Where was he serving?"

"Taiwan," Marcella replied. "No—wait. Or was it Thailand? One of those two. I'm not sure which."

CHAPTER 8

RETURN TO THE TROPICS

T he first inkling that something was wrong was a text message
from Chanya.

Problem with painting.

Already agitated by the day's events, Cornelia texted back: **What
problem?**

Thousands of miles between them not withstanding, her phone
immediately shuddered its bleak response: **Stolen.**

Cornelia had not accomplished what she'd hoped to by coming home. Miss Grace was dead, and the final visionary painting,
Apocalypse, stolen.

Nonetheless, Cornelia had learned more than she'd ever
dreamed she would. Her own grandmother was the "visionary
artist" who had allowed her own hand—as she believed—to be
a vessel for the Holy Spirit, so that it could feverishly pour out its
warnings on canvas.

Grandma had intended for Cornelia to have *Satanic Christmas*
and *Apocalypse*—one of them revealing who the Two Witnesses
were, the other one revealing their message. Grandma herself,

however, had not necessarily known the answer to either. She had only told Cornelia that the answer was "in there somewhere."

Cornelia could do nothing more in the U.S. to try to locate the stolen *Apocalypse.* If Vic and the Bangkok seller were one and the same, he might be headed back to Bangkok even now, to sell the twin to whoever wanted it so badly. Whoever wanted it so badly in addition to Cornelia, that is. And the startling theft of *Satanic Christmas* from Chanya only added to her reasons for leaving. The paintings and Miss Grace were no longer here. And even with the theft of *Apocalypse,* Cornelia had almost certainly gotten what she'd been "summoned" for: Extraordinary information about her grandmother, and her paintings. Now they were Cornelia's paintings. Except she'd managed, in the course of a single day spanning two different continents, to lose both of them. So much for her grandmother entrusting her two most precious paintings to Cornelia. Cornelia felt depressed by this, and depressed about something else: her nostalgic journey home had been a disappoint-ment. From the airport that had eradicated any trace of Christmas as effectively as an exterminator fumigates for termites, to the rot of meth labs lining Route 66, Cornelia was starting to feel as bleak about her own country—storm-ravaged and soul-ravaged—as Miss Grace had sounded in her sermons and songs.

Now, like a ping-pong ball, Cornelia was bouncing right back to Bangkok trying to track the paintings down. She also worried about what had happened to Chanya when *Satanic Christmas* was stolen. Had someone broken into his office in the slum? His office also dou-bled as his sleeping quarters, since he kept a cot in the backroom with an electric teakettle and a mini-fridge. Had he been there when it happened, working late on paperwork or sleeping? Or had he been out in the slum somewhere, attending to some emergency, which could have occurred day or night? He had provided no details in his text messaging, and when she'd tried to phone him before boarding the plane, he hadn't answered his phone. So she'd left a message and told him that with Miss Grace dead and both paintings missing, she was on her way back to Bangkok.

Now, as the plane hurtled into darkness, Cornelia shifted in her seat, craned her neck and looked around. Everyone was asleep. Occasionally, a flight attendant would slip silently past, carrying trembling plastic cups of water. Profoundly thirsty, Cornelia reached out and plucked a cup from the tray. No one else around her appeared to notice the flight attendant's offerings. Everyone else appeared deep in sleep.

What if Vic were on the plane right now?

There was no particular reason he would be, of course. Even if he were hurrying back to Thailand with his newly swiped painting, he could be taking any of a dozen airlines or flights.

Unless he was following Cornelia.

But why would he be? He'd gotten what he wanted—*Apocalypse.* She pulled out the police sketch and looked at it again. She needed to stretch her legs anyway, so she stood and started walking quietly up the aisle. A man and woman sat side-by-side wearing earphones and watching movies on the small screens on the backs of seats. One passenger was reading financial charts on a laptop computer. Nobody looked like Vic.

And then she saw him. At first, she almost walked right past him. He was fiftyish or sixtyish, she estimated, and fast asleep. He had thinning brown hair. He was also clean-shaven and wearing glasses. But if he had a few days growth of beard and hadn't been wearing glasses— could he be Vic? Cornelia wasn't sure. She looked down at him, trying to scrutinize his face in the dark airplane cabin. He stirred, and she hurried up the aisle, back to her seat.

⟞⟝ ⟞⟝

The flight attendant floated down the dark aisle like a ghost, so Cornelia stopped her and ordered a cup of coffee. She was so upset about the two missing paintings, she would never be able to fall asleep anyway. What could she do to while away the long hours without losing her mind? She opened her carry-on for a paperback and saw the letter from Miss Grace, which Marcella had given to her back in Joplin. Her heart beating faster, she turned on her overhead reading lamp.

Dearest Little Cornelia,

Let me put all of this in writing. I am starting to fret I will never see you again. I had always planned on telling you once the funeral was over and your grief had some time to heal—once you were strong enough to handle what I have been entrusted with passing on. Only, you never returned home. We haven't heard from you, and don't know where you now are. I wrote to the college in Kansas City, but they said you had gone, that you needed to "take some time and travel." This distresses me, as I have such important information to impart to you. Your grandmother, our dearest Elizabeth, was certainly the artist of the "Miss Grace Series." You know your grandmother—she surely didn't want the attention. She only felt obligated to pass on the message. The money she received from the paintings she lovingly passed on to you. But she asked me to safekeep two paintings just for you: "Satanic Christmas" and "Apocalypse." They held the secret, Elizabeth believed, to the identity of the Two End Times Witnesses and Their Warning to the World. She knew that she could trust you, her dear granddaughter, to safekeep the paintings and their message, and so you shall. Now, I must tell you one last, important thing. As Elizabeth was dying, when you were still traveling to be with her, she revealed a secret to me. She said, quite simply, "I finished the painting because I now know." Yes, in the last few weeks of her life, she had finally finished painting "Satanic Christmas." She'd painted it years before, as you know, but she'd always considered it unfinished. She believed God had something left to say. She told me once that perhaps she wasn't ready to hear it. And finally, in her last days she completed the painting. I believe it took the very last of the strength she had left. After she told me this, she handed me a slip of paper. On it she told me she had written the identity of the Two Witnesses. She gripped my hand so fiercely and told me, "Oh, Grace, we have been wrong. We have been blind." She seemed quite distressed, as was I. I did not look at the paper, as I was so stricken that she was truly dying. I only looked at it later, when I had presence of mind. By that time your grandmother was gone. I wonder now why she did not disclose this secret sooner. I believe the identity of the Two Witnesses was quite upsetting to her. If only she had told me sooner, I might have learned more. I have looked again and again at "Satanic Christmas" to try to discover what your Grandmother added. It has always looked exactly the same to me—except for one change. She painted a small crucifix at the very bottom of the painting. Your grandmother, as you know, was no Catholic, and I do not know what this means. Perhaps you will see the changes more clearly. I will write at the end of this message exactly what your grandmother divulged to me on the note. I believe she wanted you to know. So, my little Nellie, I know now I will never see you again. Godspeed and Keep Smiling.

Yours always,

Grace

And at the very end of the note, Miss Grace had written the identity of the Two Witnesses, according to Cornelia's grandmother on her deathbed:

o seth to lad of krimiov

Whatever Cornelia expected to learn from her grandmother's dying words to Miss Grace, it had certainly not been this.

CHAPTER 9

LOST IN THE SLUMS

In the bedlam of debarking, passing customs and finding baggage claim, Cornelia lost sight of the man who looked like Vic. She had caught one single glimpse of him, from a distance, as they both had entered the massive transit hall. He looked trim and scholarly—nothing like the grizzled man she saw in The Colonel's Pancake House. But the changes—a shave and glasses—were easily made. He glanced in her direction, maybe because she was openly staring at him. Then he looked away. Did he look away a little too quickly, or was she just being paranoid?

If it *were* Vic, Cornelia very much wanted to turn the tables on him and follow *him*. But her plans were interrupted by her shuddering phone. Chanya had sent a hastily typed text message:

On-ramp. Dragon. Luuk khryang. Tracks. Kittens. Clue.

What Cornelia really wanted to do was shower and fall into bed for about ten hours. But Chanya said he had a clue. Obviously, he was trying to find the painting. And although the directions wouldn't sound clear to anyone else, Cornelia knew exactly where he was talking about.

⇥+ +⇤

There are no street signs in the labyrinth of the slums. There are landmarks—such as the freeway that roars above the slum shacks, and the criss-crossing railroad tracks that carve the slum into sections. Then there are the less permanent landmarks—the kind that may or may not be there from one day to the next, like the woman with Down Syndrome who sits outside all day greeting passers-by, or the toddler and his puppy who play next to the vendor's cart selling grilled chicken and corn.

Cornelia ducked beneath the freeway on-ramp and entered the slum's narrow, twisting alleys. Squatters' shacks were built even here, with the freeway serving as a roof where heavy trucks barreled just above. The flimsy, shuddering shacks were built on stilts, and filthy, black water lapped beneath them. The slum dwellers here led precarious lives, sandwiched between concrete and canal. Cornelia paused for a moment, and sure enough, saw an ancient, reptilian creature emerge from the primeval muck. It was a komodo dragon-type creature that had somehow been surviving in this slum canal for years. The dragon was definitely on the slum dwellers' hit list, since it frequently stole eggs, chickens, cats and dogs. Some said it also stole small children. Others claimed it was only the human reptiles who did that.

Speaking of which, Cornelia turned a sharp corner in the slum and saw the *luuk khryang*, a little girl with a Thai mother and a foreign father. Chanya had been worried about sex traffickers lurking around, and had been trying to contact her Dutch father. The little girl played happily, oblivious to the danger she was in, but the older woman at her side regarded Cornelia suspiciously. Not that Cornelia blamed her. The woman had reason to be on guard against reptiles slithering through the slums.

By the time Cornelia reached the railroad tracks, she was wilting in the humidity and heat. Going back to snow-blanketed Missouri had undone her tropical acclimation completely. She paused here, and a vague uneasiness made her turn around. She caught a flash of someone ducking into a nearby alleyway. But why wouldn't there be someone behind her? This was a slum of 300,000 people that swallowed up acres along the industrial waterfront. Then Cornelia saw a litter of kittens scamper merrily across the tracks, the last landmark on Chanya's list. Chanya was obviously wandering around in this area somewhere, drawn here by a mysterious "clue." Cornelia knew this corner of the slum reasonably well, but maybe the women who worked at the noodle shop could help her find Chanya quickly. Cornelia and Chanya had shared more than one bowl of *gwayteow* here. The two women looked at Cornelia calmly as they stirred a vat of red curry and pounded furiously with bowl and pestle to make fiery *som tam*.

"Have you seen Chanya?" Cornelia asked hopefully.

"No," the taller woman replied. But she glanced quickly at the other woman, who abruptly looked away.

"He asked me to meet him here," Cornelia explained. "I thought maybe—"

The tall woman turned and began to talk with the other one, in a rapid-fire Issan dialect that Cornelia could not follow. At length, the tall woman turned back to Cornelia. "Listen," she said in a low voice. "We know who you are. We have seen you here, smiling and teaching. But we can't help you."

"What's happened?" Cornelia asked, alarmed. "Do you know where Chanya is?"

The women exchanged grave glances, then pointed straight ahead to a tiny, one-room shack. "Chanya came to visit Old

Boonsoam. And when he left Old Boonsoam's house, he seemed very excited."

"So he'll be back, then," Cornelia said. The women's expressions looked uneasy. "When did he leave?" she asked.

"That was yesterday," one of the women said sadly.

Cornelia felt like someone had socked her in the stomach. Chanya probably sent the text yesterday, but Cornelia had been on the plane and that explained the delay.

"Go talk to Old Boonsoam," the woman urged again. "He can help you." She added, "You smile like a Thai." Cornelia knew this was a compliment. A single Thai smile could communicate many different messages, from mere politeness to real menace. These women could see that Cornelia wielded her smile skillfully.

Straight ahead was Old Boonsoam's shack. It occurred to Cornelia that the last time she and Chanya had eaten at this noodle shop it had been nighttime, and they were surrounded by the din of revving motorcycle engines, raucous laughter, drinking, and conversation. Now, the slum was eerily quiet.

Old Boonsoam was a blind former monk. Being a former monk in Thailand was not unusual. Many young Thai men were Buddhist monks at least for a short while in their lives— something like a Mormon college student's mission, or a country's mandatory military service. Chanya himself had been a monk for two years. Unlike Christian monkhood, it was considered no disgrace to go for a short while, then leave. But Old Boonsoam had been a monk for many years in a remote, upcountry monastery. With no explanation, he left the much-revered monkhood to live out his last days in poverty in this sad little shack. Even though he was no longer a monk, people still venerated him and went to him for advice and help.

Boonsoam was sitting on a bamboo mat and burning incense before a statue of the Buddha when Cornelia entered. He was bare-chested and wore a threadbare blue loin cloth wrapped around his waist. The inside of the shack was dark but Boonsoam's waxen skin shone with a strange luminosity. He was bald as a cue ball and appeared matchstick frail, as if a gust of wind could extinguish him. His dark, almost black eyes stared straight ahead, unseeing.

"Yes?" he called, upon hearing Cornelia enter.

Even though Boonsoam was blind, Cornelia still tried to sit appropriately for a woman in Thailand, her legs tucked modestly to one side. She had an inexplicable sensation that Boonsoam could still see her.

"Khruu Boonsoam," she said. She didn't think she should address him as a monk, so she decided to settle on "Teacher." She only hoped this wasn't insulting to him. She folded her hands and bowed respectfully.

"Who are you?" he asked. "A foreigner who speaks Thai?"

"Yes," she said. "I am Khun Cornelia."

Instantly, Old Boonsoam leaned forward, alert.

"Khun Chanya's friend," he whispered. "The smiling teacher. He told me you would come."

"Yes," Cornelia said. "Khun Chanya's friend. And the women outside—" She gestured uselessly, since he was blind. "They told me he came here to talk with you just before he left. And that was yesterday." She tried to keep the worry out of her voice. "What did you talk about?"

"About the witness," Old Boonsoam said.

Cornelia's pulse quickened. "What witness?"

"A man upcountry and across the river in Laos. He claims to be one of...two witnesses."

"How did Chanya find him?" Cornelia wondered in surprise.

"He has a website," Old Boonsoam said.

"The witness has a website?"

"Yes," Old Boonsoam nodded. "Chanya found the website while researching the...Two Witnesses. I understand it's from the Christian scriptures? Yes?"

Cornelia nodded, and then remembered Boonsoam was blind. "Yes."

"Chanya came to ask me about this man. He was right to come. I know him well."

"You *know* him?"

"Oh, yes. We were brother monks, once. And now neither of us is," he remarked. Was it Cornelia's imagination, or was his voice wistful?

"What happened?" Cornelia asked gingerly. She wasn't sure if she was asking what happened to Boonsoam or to the other monk.

"Brother Lek left the monastery," Old Boonsoam said simply. "He felt he had a special mission. He lived in the woods as a hermit, fasting and meditating. He was also very busy sculpting."

"Sculpting?"

"Yes. He made very many sculptures out of stone. They grew up all around him, these sculptures. It was like his dreams were turned into stone. Brother Lek believed these stone visions held a deep secret, a special message, bigger than he was. A terrible and ancient mystery. After a while, he began to draw...devotees. Followers. Some said he had healing powers."

Outside, Cornelia heard the wind kick up, causing a sheet metal door to bang repeatedly.

"Is someone there?" Boonsoam called, his voice quavering. "I hear someone outside."

Cornelia glanced out the open doorway, perplexed. "It's just the wind," she said. She leaned forward. "Khruu Boonsoam. Do you believe in Brother Lek's healing powers?"

"I don't know," Boonsoam said. "I am blind. I never saw his sculptures. I did feel some of them, with my hands. They had a... strange energy. Brother Lek even tried to heal me of my blindness once. But as you can see, he failed."

"A Buddhist as one of the Two Witnesses?" Cornelia murmured. She was thinking out loud.

"Brother Lek has carved out his own belief," Old Boonsoam said reflectively. "He has sculpted his own temple out of stone."

"Do you think Chanya went to see him?" Cornelia asked. She touched her throat, nervously fingering the locket which contained her father's portrait.

"Yes, Chanya seemed very worried about a painting he'd lost. He said it belonged to you, and he had to get it back. He told me the painting was about the Two Witnesses, so he was very surprised to learn from this website that one of the Witnesses claimed to be living in Laos," Boonsoam said. "Chanya thought perhaps Brother Lek might have information about your painting. Or a *lead* of some sort, as he put it. Brother Lek's stone garden is in Laos. Across the river from where our monastery was."

"Brother Lek," Cornelia repeated. "It means *small*. That's my last name."

"Yes," Boonsoam said. "Our small brother. He was an American, just like you. He came to the monastery as a young man after the Vietnam War."

"Why did he take the name Brother Lek?" Cornelia prodded. "Was he...small? Or—"

Old Boonsoam cocked his head and looked faintly amused. "Small? Being blind, I'm not the best judge."

Just then, Cornelia's cell phone vibrated. She glanced down at Chanya's text message: **Stay put. Hot on trail. Will call soon.**

CHAPTER 10

DEATH ON THE NIGHT TRAIN

C ornelia had one photograph of her grandfather. In the photograph, the sun was shining, he was smiling, and leaning
against his car, a 1963 Jaguar XKE convertible. Color: British
Racing Green. He was a "car man," her grandmother always said.

"We both had good jobs and no children," she explained, when
Cornelia asked why they hadn't kept such a nice car. "Of course,
your father would soon be on the way. So he had to sell the car."

The year was 1964. Her grandparents were newly married, and
they'd just bought their first car. They lived in a garage apartment
on a quiet street in Joplin. This photograph of her grandfather
was taken when his adult life was new and his future unwritten.
It also was taken on the brink of cataclysmic change. Cornelia's
father was about to be conceived—and her grandfather was about
to be drafted. He would be swept up in the momentum of the
Vietnam War, from which he would never return. Not even his
body. Cornelia and her grandfather would never meet.

Or at least that's what she'd always assumed.

The loudspeaker announced, in Thai, the departure of Cornelia's
train to Nong Khai. Chanya's message not withstanding, of course

65

she couldn't stay put. A second-class ticket cost her $15, which bought her a private, curtained berth with a reading light, pillow and blanket. With no fanfare or whistles, the train lurched away. Vendors walked through the train crying out melodiously, *"Nam laaw bier,"* or "Water and beer!" Squid-on-a-stick and sticky rice were also available. Cornelia had her grandfather's photograph, Miss Grace's letter, and a Bible spread out on her berth.

They grew up all around him, these sculptures. Brother Lek believed these stones held a deep secret, a special message, bigger than he was. A terrible and ancient mystery. They had a...strange energy. After a while, he began to draw...devotees. Some said he had healing powers.

Brother Lek's name meant Small, which was Cornelia's last name. He was a young American who arrived at the monastery at the end of the Vietnam War. Her grandfather's body was never recovered. And Brother Lek seemed to be...a visionary artist, just like Cornelia's grandmother—his wife. Was it all just coincidence? Strangest of all, he said he was one of the Two Witnesses—and Cornelia's grandmother had painted a prophetic picture about their identity. Who was this Brother Lek? And Cornelia's own grandmother and grandfather—who were they, really?

Cornelia glanced out the window, where all was darkness. Cornelia had visited Nong Khai Province before. She had taken a riverboat ride from there up the Mekong River into Laos. She had become good friends with the Laotian boat owner whose name was Pin-Pon. Now the train rumbled through jungle, then valley, then mountains. A milk-white Buddha statue loomed up and flashed past like a giant, hulking ghost. The hubbub of the train's initial departure had died down. Most of the eating, drinking and talking had dissipated. Passengers now dozed in their berths. Occasionally, Cornelia's curtain would rustle as someone brushed past in the aisle.

This photograph had never seemed so precious to her. It was her only means of proving whether or not "Brother Lek" was her own grandfather. Fifty years had passed, of course—but still. There was a chance she could look at Brother Lek and know instantly whether he was the same man who was in her photograph. And Brother Lek could certainly take one look at the photograph and recognize instantly whether or not he was her grandfather. So many questions crowded her mind, but one pierced repeatedly through the fog of shock and confusion. If Brother Lek were her grandfather—*why had he never come home?* Answering this question was far more urgent to Cornelia than whether or not he was one of the "Two Witnesses."

Unless, of course, that was exactly why he'd never come home. Had something happened to him during the war that had forever altered his course? After his helicopter was shot down, when he was wounded and lost in the jungle—what had he seen? What had he heard? What had happened that led him to disappear for fifty years? Maybe he had lost his memory after the crash, and constructed an entirely new identity from scratch. Maybe he'd forgotten who he was in an earlier life—but couldn't escape it completely. Cornelia looked down at her grandmother's last message.

o seth to lad of krimiov

This, she had claimed on her death bed, revealed the identity of the Two Witnesses. It meant absolutely nothing to Cornelia. Her grandfather's name was Daniel, not Seth. Their last name was Small, not Krimiov. She had never heard of any person or any place named "Krimiov," although it sounded vaguely Russian. She certainly wasn't, so far as she knew, Russian.

Cornelia reached for the pocket Bible she'd picked up in Joplin. She slipped the photograph and letter inside the Bible, slipped the Bible back inside her knapsack, and pulled her curtain aside, peeking into the aisle. The train rocked and rolled along, but the aisle was empty and silent. Cornelia wanted to stay awake, but jet lag was stalking her. It was time for some coffee. She pulled herself out of her berth and wobbled down the aisle, knapsack slung over one shoulder, toward the dining car.

"Dining car" was too grand a name for the rear car where a cook fried up greasy Thai food surrounded by smoking woks and hot chili oil. Sitting there caused her eyes to sting and her throat to close. The menu offered fried rice with shrimp, or pork with chili peppers and basil, or a bowl of rice soup generously splashed with hot sauce.

Cornelia took a stool and ordered a cup of Thai coffee, both bitter and sweet. So much of Thailand—its sights, its smells, its sounds—brought extremes, not into balance, but into collision. At least that was how Cornelia experienced Thailand—as jarring, and disorienting. But maybe for the Buddhist Thais, the collision of extremes was cathartic, and led to the calm after the storm.

She phoned Chanya for the hundredth time, but he wasn't answering. She hadn't yet informed him that she was on her way. Cornelia knew he wouldn't approve—but this was about much more than a painting now. She had never talked about her grandfather with Chanya, but now she wanted desperately to talk about her grandfather, every detail she could dredge up—and Brother Lek. Cornelia sighed without realizing it, causing the two men sitting at the other end of the counter, murmuring and drinking Mekong whiskey, to look up.

Was her grandfather dead or alive? And if he was one of the Two Witnesses, what was his message? Did this "stone vision" that had been carved out of the jungle contain the same warning that was supposedly painted on the *Apocalypse* painting? Why was this warning so important, important enough that he'd abandoned his wife and son, and never returned home?

Cornelia glanced out the window, where the mountains had given way to a wide, thirsty plain. In the middle of nowhere, a gas station loomed up and floated by, a shining, modern island quickly swallowed by the tropical night. She wondered now what exactly her grandmother had painted on the canvas of *Apocalypse*. This was supposedly the message the Witnesses had come to proclaim. Cornelia remembered the feeling she'd had driving through the darkness of the American heartland and listening to Miss Grace singing out admonitions and prayers to her country. No matter how far Miss Grace believed they'd strayed, no matter how pagan she thought they'd become—even to the point of de-Christianizing Christmas—that night Cornelia felt immensely comforted that there were still Miss Graces left in America. Maybe those few flickering flames like Miss Grace, scattered across a map of darkness, had a purifying effect— maybe the holy presence of a few meant entire cities would survive as well. What about the story of Jonah and Ninevah? Hadn't the people listened to the warning and averted destruction? And what was the story of Sodom and Gomorrah? That as long as there were ten good men left in a city, it wouldn't be destroyed?

But Miss Grace was gone.

The voice on the airwaves was the voice of a ghost. What if all the Miss Graces had been supplanted by meth dealers? What if there weren't even ten good men left? Cornelia tried to ignore the next question that suddenly arose in her mind:

Or what if there's only you?

But I'm not holy, Cornelia thought bleakly. If anyone is depending on me, they're in big trouble.

The men drinking whiskey had already retired. The cook had disappeared. No one else was around. Clutching the Bible to her side, Cornelia staggered through the swaying train back to her berth.

She collapsed inside, pulling her curtain tight. Criss-crossing oceans and resurrecting old ghosts had exhausted her. She cupped her hand over her silver locket, and with her father's portrait close to her heart, she fell asleep.

Once, in the small hours of the night, she awoke. The train had paused for some inexplicable reason. When she looked out the window, she saw a full moon and a shimmering monastery in the stillness. Its ornamental, curving roof glittered like gold. Through the thin curtain, she also thought she saw a shadow lingering in the aisle beside her berth. She stirred and yanked the curtain open, but caught only a glimpse of a closing door as someone disappeared into the next car. Maybe it had been a porter making the rounds.

Bright sun poured into Cornelia's berth as the train groaned to a halt. Outside, she could see the bustle of the Nong Khai train station. A knot of tuk-tuk drivers waited eagerly for passengers to de-board. Suddenly, a woman screamed. Cornelia threw back her curtain and stepped into the aisle—and into bedlam.

A man lay face-down only a few feet away.

"*Khaw ben farang!*" someone shouted. He's a foreigner!

A porter pushed his way through the mob and knelt down, fingers to the man's neck.

"*Yong my die,*" the man whispered. He's not dead yet. Abruptly, the porter stood and looked frantically around. He pushed through the crowd and hurried down the aisle.

"*Khun Pa yew nee,*" a passenger said. There's a priest on board.

In a few moments, the priest appeared. He was a big Caucasian man, obviously a *farang*.

"Is he Catholic?" the priest asked, as he knelt down. "What happened to him?"

My rue, people shrugged. I don't know. There was no blood, Cornelia noticed. Did he have a heart attack?

The priest reached into the man's pockets, presumably for identification, and pulled out a train ticket stub. *Berth 237.* The priest grasped the man by the shoulder, turning him slightly to see his face. Cornelia almost gasped out loud, and the priest also looked startled. It was Vic, the man who'd been drinking coffee in Wrigley's Store the night she'd arrived in Newton, and who'd followed her later that night. It was the man who'd stolen *Apocalypse* from Marcella at the storage locker.

The priest made the sign of the cross over the man and appeared to be praying. Poor Vic was apparently dead. Horrified, Cornelia backed away. This man whom she'd never even met, who'd been haunting her like a ghost—now really was one. The door behind her swung open, and a medic along with two policemen entered the train car, pushing past Cornelia to reach Vic. Cornelia decided to exit through the swinging door and escape the growing hubbub. Once she was inside the adjoining train car, she paused for a moment in the sudden stillness, trying to collect her thoughts. Then she realized Berth 237 was directly above her. Cornelia looked around cautiously, but this train car was quiet as a tomb. All the activity was in the next car. She climbed up the ladder, pulled back the curtain, and looked inside. It had been a long shot, but she'd hoped *Apocalypse* might be sitting right there for her to find. The berth was empty.

"Find anything interesting?"

Startled, Cornelia almost fell off the ladder. Standing at the bottom, arms folded, was the priest. *Keep your composure,* her grandmother commanded sternly.

Cornelia smiled. "Father, I was looking for the *Apocalypse.*"

This time it was the priest who nearly fell down.

CHAPTER 11

THE WALLS OF THE RECTORY

Father Bill's hands shook as he offered Cornelia a cup of coffee. The cup rattled in its saucer as he set it down on the table top.

"I have a tremor in my hand," he said apologetically. "I've always had it."

An unfinished Scrabble game was laid out on the table. Cornelia noticed the words *witness, icon,* and *visionary.* Also, *locution.*

"I play when I'm alone," Father Bill noted. "To keep my mind sharp." A ghost of a smile flitted across his face. "You'll understand when you get older." He watched Cornelia intently as she spooned milk into her coffee cup. "I just got back from a meeting in Bangkok," he explained. "That's why I was on the train."

He was in his sixties, Cornelia guessed. He was tall and broad-shouldered and gray-haired with fierce blue eyes. Unsmiling, he appeared formidable, even intimidating, like someone who would not allow any obstacle to impede his progress. Which was why the walls of his house—the rectory, as he called it—were so strange.

"So," he said, looking closely at Cornelia. "You are the granddaughter of Miss Grace."

Cornelia choked on the coffee she was sipping. When she'd told Father Bill that her grandmother had painted *Apocalypse,* and that's why she was looking for it in a dead man's berth, she'd forgotten that nobody knew her grandmother was the real artist—nobody except for her and Marcella, that is. It occurred to her now that Father Bill might not believe her story. To him, she'd appear an opportunist, a gold digger, a charlatan.

"Well," Cornelia hesitated.

"I've read a lot of articles about your grandmother and her art. She's always been described as...devoted to her craft. Obsessed with it, even. So focused on it that she never married. Or had children. I believe one article called her a southern spinster." He smiled broadly—it was a humorless smile—and rocked back in his chair. "It's true that when I went there on home leave to procure *Satanic Christmas*, your grandmother had already passed away. But I've seen pictures of her. Of Miss Grace." He gazed levelly at Cornelia. "She didn't resemble you at all. More coffee?"

"My grandmother painted *Satanic Christmas* and *Apocalypse*," Cornelia repeated serenely.

Abruptly, Father Bill leaned forward. "How did you learn about the missing twin, *Apocalypse*?"

"Because," Cornelia said, still smiling. "I'm the granddaughter." Father Bill was intimidating, and he was trying to intimidate Cornelia. He mistook her slight build and feminine smile for an easy target. Like Thais who had smiles for every occasion, Cornelia also had a smile repertoire. Sometimes, her smile could be deceiving. It wasn't planned or deliberate. Her smiles sprang from deep inside her—they were organic.

"It seemed like a miracle when I obtained *Satanic Christmas*," Father Bill said, sounding nostalgic. "I wasn't even sure it actually existed. No one was. There were just rumors of two lost paintings." He closed his eyes. "All I did was show up on Miss Grace's front porch to ask about them. I offered to buy them. Others had tried, of course, and been turned away by her. It turned out I had just missed her. She had just passed away. Her nephew answered the door. They were going through her things, settling her estate. He told me he would sell me a painting called *Satanic Christmas*, that it would cover the costs of her burial and so forth." Father Bill opened his eyes and gazed at Cornelia, his expression opaque. "I couldn't believe my good fortune. I was dumbfounded. He had two conditions. I had to pay cash, and I had to take it and go immediately. He seemed very anxious for me to leave."

"Frank," Cornelia sighed. "He knew Marcella wouldn't agree to selling it, so he had to act right away."

"Before I left, I asked him about the twin to *Satanic Christmas*. I told him I would buy it as well. But a woman started calling to him from another room, and he shut the door on me without answering."

"Unfortunately," Cornelia continued. "*Apocalypse* is still missing. Thanks to Victor Whatever-his-name-was. No disrespect to him intended, but he stole *Apocalypse* from me and made a real mess of things before he died." Cornelia offered her own version of the Thai "fun yim" smile: *I'm smiling but I sure don't mean it.*

"You're very calm in lieu of what's happened," Father Bill said, offering a chilly smile in return. It was as if they had each unsheathed their smiles and were doing battle. The more warmth Cornelia radiated, the icier Father Bill's smile became in return. Whose smile would eclipse whose?

"That man's name was Victor Bilge," Father Bill said. "And he was a decent soul. Not perfect, but who is? He lived in a nearby village for years with his Thai wife. Most foreign men take the Thai women out of their own culture and force them to adapt to their Western lives. He was one of the few I've ever met who stayed and assimilated completely into his wife's village life. He was as fluent in Thai as anyone I've ever met. Some foreigners with Thai wives never do learn to talk to their wives. Victor came around here periodically just to talk to a fellow American." Father Bill fell silent for a moment, gazing past Cornelia. "He wasn't even Catholic," he added absently. "But that didn't matter. Ex-pats like to gather together. Strangers in a strange land." Father Bill abruptly laughed. "He liked to have a drink with me and talk about golf. Of course, neither of us had actually golfed in decades."

"And you gave *Satanic Christmas* to him?" Cornelia asked.

Father Bill looked genuinely surprised. "Of course not," he said. "Tragically, somebody stole—" He stopped mid-sentence. Then he looked soberly at Cornelia. "You think Vic was the one who stole the painting from me?"

"Paintings," Cornelia reminded him. "Plural. Vic may have been great at assimilating into Thai culture—but he was also very expert at stealing my grandmother's paintings."

"How do you know?" Father Bill demanded.

"I found *Satanic Christmas* in a shop in Bangkok. It had been sold to them by some American from upcountry whose Thai wife had just died."

Father Bill looked disappointed. "That sounds like Vic," he admitted. "He knew about *Satanic Christmas*, of course. It was hanging right here in my house. Along with all the other paintings. As you can see, I'm a collector."

That was an understatement. Father Bill's small house—next door to the church where he was the pastor—was covered in religious art. Jesus, Mary, sometimes both of them together, seemed to be watching from every nook and cranny. It made Cornelia uncomfortable, and it took her a moment to realize why. The aura of this rectory, of these walls, of this collection was *obsessive*. Cornelia knew little about art, and had forgotten much of her Christianity, but she recognized these classic depictions of Jesus Christ and his mother came from the Catholic world, which would explain Father Bill's devotion to collecting them. They crowded the walls, leaving no space to breathe. The Protestant Christian world Cornelia had grown up in hadn't reveled in all these ancient, vivid images of Jesus floating around. Too much art—even of Jesus—smacked of idolatry.

But there were other pictures on Father Bill's wall, and they weren't old paintings. They were photographs—some black-and-white and grainy, some more recent color photographs. The photographs were very strange, as well. For one thing, the photographs were of children. And something about the children's expressions troubled Cornelia profoundly.

Another odd thing she noticed about Father Bill's rectory walls—there were no outsider paintings. *Satanic Christmas* must have been the only visionary art he had owned. Why?

"Vic had never seemed too interested in any of my art before," Father Bill said, sounding puzzled. "But he did quiz me about *Satanic Christmas* not too long ago. It was because he'd heard about Brother Lek's latest escapades. Brother Lek has been a fixture around here for years, of course. That is to say, we've all heard about him. Not many have seen him, though. I never have. He's been in seclusion behind those compound walls for years. With the spread of the internet, though, he has become something of a P.R. guru. Publishing his writings. Photographs of his sculptures. All with a *Donate* button, of course. No photographs of him, though. Anyway, recently he's really gone off the deep end. Claiming to be one of the Two Witnesses and all that." Father Bill sighed. "One day Vic just seemed to put two and two together. He was staring at *Satanic Christmas* and he said, out of the blue: "Did you know Brother Lek claims to be one of those witnesses?" Father Bill frowned. "I didn't think much of it then. But I guess Vic had his eye on the painting. Maybe he thought Brother Lek would be interested in buying the painting. Vic had been really struggling since his wife died. Started drinking and gambling quite a bit. I think he'd run up some debts." He drummed his fingers on the table top. "I wonder what he was doing on the train."

Cornelia wondered, too. Had he still been following her? Maybe he'd been following her since she'd left the plane—in the slum, when she was visiting Old Boonsoam, and slipping past her sleeping berth in the middle of the night on the train. Since he'd heard her conversation at Wrigley's Store in Newton, he'd known she was on the trail of the twin paintings—one that he'd already stolen and sold in Bangkok, the second that he would steal in Joplin after eavesdropping on Cornelia. He had planned to sell *Apocalypse* as well, she assumed. But why continue following Cornelia? Because he thought she might be willing to pay to get *Apocalypse* back if his other customers didn't work out? Possibly. Because he thought Cornelia might have even more Miss Grace treasures that he could profit from, that he had stumbled onto a mother lode? Also possible.

Something else was bothering Cornelia. "You said that Brother Lek has gone off the deep end?" she asked cautiously. Was the grandfather she was finally going to meet completely crazy? Was he lost like Kurtz in his own heart of darkness? Or was he so holy that he was one of the two most important actors in the End Times? And most importantly to Cornelia—was he really her long-lost grandfather? "But you've never seen Brother Lek? Not even his picture?" If so, it would be useless to show Father Bill the photograph of her grandfather.

"No, I've never seen him," Father Bill said. "I believe his disappearing act is partly deliberate, to create a sense of mystery. To attract disciples. He's quite shrewd, I think. Of course, he may also just be a bit mad." He looked at her curiously. "I wonder why Vic didn't sell *Satanic Christmas* to Brother Lek. Why did he take it to that Bangkok shop?"

"Maybe Brother Lek—" Cornelia swallowed hard because she almost said *my grandfather.* "Maybe Brother Lek didn't want to pay for it. Or he didn't want to pay enough to suit Vic."

"Maybe," Father Bill agreed. His expression darkened. "Now what is this about Vic also stealing *Apocalypse?*"

Cornelia filled Father Bill in on the ongoing saga of her grand-mother's two "lost paintings." Now both really were lost, thanks largely to Vic.

"So you're telling me that Miss Grace was the front man for your grandmother, the actual artist?" Father Bill said.

"That's one way of putting it," Cornelia said.

Father Bill looked at Cornelia thoughtfully. "That's a pretty elaborate ruse to carry on for years and years," he said softly. "No offense, but it sounds far-fetched to me."

Cornelia was just about to pull out Miss Grace's letter when Father Bill spoke up.

"O.K.," he said. "So Vic stole *Satanic Christmas* from me hoping to peddle it to Brother Lek. For whatever reason, Brother Lek wasn't interested—not in Vic's price, maybe, or not in the content of the painting. So instead Vic sold it to the store in Bangkok, seemingly under pressure to unload it for financial and possibly other reasons—because, according to the shop-keeper, he seemed afraid someone was on his trail." The priest frowned. "Was he worried about me putting two and two together and reporting him to the police? Or was he anxious about someone else's interest in the painting? Was he afraid of those he owed money to? Whatever the answer, that's where you rescued it and handed it over to your friend for safekeeping. Vic heads off for America in search of Miss Grace's homestead and the lost twin. But this is what I don't understand."

Then Father Bill asked a question that stopped Cornelia cold.

"*Who stole* **Satanic Christmas** *from your friend who was keeping it safe for you?* I mean—why would Vic steal the same painting *twice*? Besides, wasn't he still in the U.S. when *Satanic Christmas* was stolen from your friend?"

Cornelia had no answer for that. *Was* someone else hunting down her grandmother's paintings as well? She thought of the American woman who had expressed interest in *Satanic Christmas* in Bangkok.

"*Apocalypse* wasn't with him on the train either," Cornelia murmured. "Unless—" Unless someone—like the American wife—had beaten Cornelia to it. But it would be an impossible coincidence that someone else who was interested in the painting also happened to be on the train, saw that Vic had died, and stole the painting from his berth. Unless—Cornelia had a disturbing thought. Unless Vic's death hadn't been natural, and whoever took the painting *caused* the death. She immediately had another, equally disturbing thought. What if Brother Lek decided he wanted *Satanic Christmas* after all, but didn't want to pay for it? Maybe he had stolen *Satanic Christmas* from Chanya. Maybe he had also stolen *Apocalypse*—after murdering Vic on the night train. Cornelia's gaze wandered back to the cluttered walls where she noticed, among the pictures and paintings, a crucifix.

"You saw *Satanic Christmas*," Cornelia said. "Why do you think my grandmother painted a crucifix on it? She wasn't Catholic."

Father Bill looked puzzled. "A crucifix? Do you mean the rosary?"

The phone on the wall emitted a shrill ring. Father Bill stood and reached for it. Cornelia stirred her cold instant coffee out of sheer nervousness. She wanted to quiz Father Bill more about Brother Lek. She wanted to go see Brother Lek as quickly as possible.

Father Bill was speaking Thai, but Cornelia could understand every word. Perhaps he didn't realize that. In any event, Father Bill was telling the police that yes, he knew who Cornelia Small was. Apparently, they'd been trying to track her down since she'd left the train with Father Bill. But how, Cornelia wondered, had the police connected Cornelia with Vic? She had given no indication when his body was discovered that she knew who he was. She'd slipped away from the tumult to look into Vic's sleeping berth, hoping to recover her stolen paintings. Only Father Bill had noticed Cornelia and followed—or so she'd thought.

"You think he was murdered?" Father Bill said, sounding shocked. He turned and looked straight at Cornelia, his blue eyes blazing, his expression unreadable. "I don't know. Maybe she *can* be of some help." He turned away from Cornelia and continued talking. But by the time he hung up the phone, Cornelia was gone.

CHAPTER 12
RIVER CROSSING

I am not a fugitive, Cornelia repeated to herself sternly. She was crouched down low in a wooden long-tail boat wearing a conical straw hat like the rice farmers wore in the fields. To anyone watching, she'd look exactly like any other Laotian farmer. Except, perhaps, for the cell phone she kept furtively checking in case Chanya had called. The boat sliced expertly across the muddy currents of the Mekong, from the Thai side to the Lao side, as approaching storm clouds darkened the afternoon sky. Red and blue ribbons fluttered from the bow to pay respects to the spirits of the water. Cornelia's old friend Pin-Pon was at the helm.

"To your favorite guest house in Vientiane?" he queried. Typically taciturn, he offered her a sudden, sunny smile. It occurred to Cornelia that he was happy to see her.

"Yes," Cornelia agreed. "I want to surprise a friend who's there. I thought this would be a fun way to arrive and greet him." Cornelia felt a pang of guilt at how easily she lied to Pin-Pon. "Of course, when it's time to return to Thailand, I'll need another ride back since I won't have a visa stamp." At least that much was true.

"Yes," Pin-Pon agreed gravely, his smile flickering. "You could get in a lot of trouble if you get caught entering Thailand without your exit and re-entry stamp." He sounded a tad disapproving, Cornelia thought. Pin-Pon's figure was lean and muscular against the darkening sky, and an aura of mystery emanated from his dark eyes and finely chiseled features.

"And so could you," she added guiltily.

Pin-Pon laughed. "I make many trips, licit and illicit. Sometimes, I must pay bribes for these trips. Some trips are for friends, some for acquaintances, both Thai and Lao. They have something honest to sell, or to buy, or someone to visit, or somewhere to work. But I don't like to transport foreigners illegally, no matter how much they pay—and they pay very well. Usually a foreigner who wants to cross illegally is up to no good." Pin-Pon looked around cautiously and lowered his voice. "There are things, you know, that are being transported. Bad things. *Death.* Drugs. Guns. Women. Even the trafficking of–" He hesitated. "*Children.*" He poled the wooden boat gently through a swirling current and looked down at Cornelia, his eyes opaque. "But I know you, Cornelia. You do not work to harm those children. You work to help them in that monstrous slum. You do not traffic in death. So I will help you. With me, you are safe. And right now, you are just a poor woman from Laos who is returning home after a long day's work for a higher wage in *Myanthai.*" Pin-Pon stood in the rear of the boat, poling his way across the river, his handsome face shining. He seemed a bit otherworldly, almost like a ghost. Two people fishing from a wooden boat drifted along in the center of the river, and the Laotian flag rippled in the cool breeze that was stirring the palm trees. A dinner cruise nosed its way along the Thai side of the bank, blaring Issan folk tunes. Cornelia could smell the pungent chili oil and the sizzling meat and the fragrant aroma of jasmine rice as a delectable Thai dinner was dished up on the boat.

I did not flee from the Thai police, she reminded herself again, burning with guilt over Pin-Pon's trust. *If they ask, I'll play dumb. Father Bill doesn't know I understand Thai. I didn't give him any opportunity to tell me that the police wanted to talk to me. I'll tell them I received a cell phone call and I had to leave immediately. That could have happened.*

"Did you hear the big news?" Pin-Pon asked. "That a foreigner was murdered on the train?"

Cornelia was grateful that her head was down and the hat covered her face. "Oh, really?" she murmured, turning off her cell phone and slipping it into her knapsack. The battery was getting low, and still no word from Chanya. "Where's he from?"

And why do the police think I can help? What information do they possibly think I might have?

"How did you know it was a "he?" Pin-Pon asked, glancing sharply down at her.

"Oh-well, I assumed a man got killed in a fight," Cornelia quickly replied. "A drunk man. A drunk tourist. Maybe over a woman." *Shut up!* she berated herself. *You've already said too much.*

"Yes, a woman," Pin-Pon murmured vaguely. "A foreign woman. But it wasn't a fight. They believe he was killed with durian."

"What?" Cornelia cried, looking up and nearly knocking her straw hat off in the process. "Killed with durian?" Durian was a football-sized fruit that smelled so much like dirty socks it was banned from trains and buses.

Pin-Pon gazed down on Cornelia pensively. "You know how it's done," he said neutrally. "Durian is a hot fruit, and one must never, never mix it with alcohol. Someone served our *farang* a blend of Mekong whiskey and durian juice."

Thais distinguished between hot fruit and cool fruit in a way that mystified Cornelia. A Thai once told Cornelia that whether or not a fruit was "hot" or "cool" had to do with how it felt inside one's stomach—a sensation both other-worldly and down-to-earth. Again, it was that explosive combination of extremes—heat colliding with cold, in fruits, in spices, in stomachs and hearts. Durian was a particularly potent "hot" fruit that was supposedly lethal when mixed with alcohol. "I thought that was an old wives' tale," Cornelia said.

"Old wives?" Pin-Pon repeated.

"You know. An urban legend," Cornelia explained.

"Urban legend?"

"Never mind. Are they sure that's what killed him?" she asked, still skeptical. "Cyanide, maybe. Arsenic. But *durian?*"

"Poison is their suspicion," Pin-Pon said darkly. "But they are investigating."

"Maybe they think it was a robbery?" Cornelia suggested. "Was something stolen?"

"Maybe it was robbery," Pin-Pon agreed. "Perhaps he was carrying something of value. Of course, only a native could have committed the crime. Only a native, after all, would know how to concoct such a deadly drink." He glanced down at Cornelia, but in the gathering gloom she couldn't read his expression.

Then why were the police looking for me? Cornelia wondered, once again. She was on her way to Brother Lek's stone garden in Laos. But she had entered illegally across the river because she had been afraid to openly cross the bridge using her own name and passport. She was afraid she'd be stopped by the Thai police, that they were indeed looking for her.

"Here we are," Pin-Pon murmured, as the warm lights of the guest-house slid into view. He and Cornelia both craned their necks and peered upward, where the thatched bamboo walls of the Mekong Guest House teetered precariously at the top of a steep riverbank. A long flight of crumbling stone steps led from the shore of the Mekong River up to the guesthouse. Cornelia bowed her head for a moment, thoughtful.

Maybe the police aren't looking for information from me, she finally admitted to herself. *Maybe they've learned about the murdered man's involvement with the stolen paintings and—death by durian or not—it's me they suspect.*

CHAPTER 13

MEKONG MYSTERY

The guesthouse owner, a tall, gaunt British man named Ian, brought Cornelia a Tiger Beer. The beer hadn't been refrigerated—it was poured at room temperature into a glass full of ice. His Laotian wife Lily, who was fat and beaming and spoke with a perfect British accent, set down a dish of peanuts mixed with green onions, salt, hot peppers and lime.

"Have you heard the news?" Ian asked, sliding his long legs into a chair at the polished bamboo table where Cornelia sat beneath a thatched roof and lazy ceiling fan. She glanced down at her phone once again, hoping for a text from Chanya. The background image on her phone was of her grandmother's old house in Newton, which Cornelia had snapped while visiting. The two-story brick house once served as an inn which housed Union soldiers during the Civil War. *The Valley Inn*, it was called. Cornelia felt a pang of sorrow about everything—that she'd lost her grandmother, lost her home, and now lost the two paintings which were all she'd had left of her past.

Nearby, a smattering of backpackers read paperbacks, scrolled through their phones, or dozed in hammocks which hung from coconut and banana trees. Cornelia had no desire to spend any time

in her room. It had a cot and a fan and reeked of chemical mosquito repellent, which was plugged into the wall and warmed up like
electric air freshener. The walls of her room were bamboo-thin
and the bathhouse was communal, but she couldn't complain—it
cost her $6.

Cornelia had a sweeping view of the swirling waters of the muddy Mekong, and she pretended to enjoy that view now.

"What news is that?" she asked, trying her best to sound
bored.

"Murder on the night train!" Ian declared dramatically. "An
American! Why, I've never heard of such a thing! Some petty
theft, maybe, on the train, perhaps a bit of sexual harassment.
But the murder of a foreigner?" Ian made a clucking noise with
his tongue and shook his head ruefully. "The Thai government
is not going to like this, not one little bit." Cornelia continued to stare at the churning waters of the Mekong. Too late,
Cornelia realized that her unresponsiveness had led Ian to scrutinize Cornelia closely. "I'm surprised the news hasn't already
spread like wildfire through the ex-pat community over there
in Thailand."

"Oh!" Cornelia said, pretending to be startled. "You mean the
killing of the tourist? That's right, I heard something, but no details. So it was on the *night train*? And he was an *American*?" Cornelia
shook her head. "That *is* shocking."

"He was no tourist!" Lily chortled.

Cornelia glanced sharply at Lily. "Did you know him?" she
asked.

"Not personally," she laughed. "But I have family who live
across the river. They knew him very well. He had lived with his
Thai wife for years in a village not far from Nong Khai. She had
died recently and he had begun drinking and gambling. He left
the village some time ago, reportedly deep in debt. Maybe he was
fleeing those to whom he owed money."

Maybe, Cornelia silently agreed. Perhaps that's who he was afraid of in Bangkok, in addition to the police, after Father Bill reported the stolen painting.

"But here's the oddest part," Ian said in a low voice. He looked around carefully, as if one of the backpackers might be eavesdropping. "He left the Thai village and his debts and reportedly fled to America. Then, for some reason, *he decided to come back.* Now, why would he do that?" Ian leaned back and looked triumphantly at Cornelia. Obviously, he already had an answer to his own question.

"I don't know," Cornelia admitted. It was a good question. "Why?"

Lily picked up the narrative. "Because he had supposedly obtained something in America. Something *priceless*, to pay his gambling debt with. He had written to his wife's family in the village, informing them of this news."

"Did he tell his in-laws what the priceless object was?" Cornelia asked, trying to conceal her own agitation.

Ian spread his hands and shrugged. "Nobody seems to know. But whatever it was, it went missing after the murder. Nothing of any value was found on him or in his sleeping berth. But a porter and some other passengers confirm he was carrying a somewhat bulky package with him when he entered his sleeping berth. No one saw him leave for the rest of the night."

"But the next morning, someone"—here Lily glanced at Cornelia—"a *foreigner* found his body. Now they think that foreigner—*a woman*—killed him for his fortune. A wandering drug addict, perhaps. Addicted to *yaa baa*." Methamphetamines. The crazy drug.

"That *is* odd," Cornelia said. "That a female tourist would kill a...male tourist." She could feel herself perspiring and hoped Ian and Lily would attribute it to the spices and the sultry night.

"And completely ridiculous," Ian said dismissively. "A story concocted by the Thai government to protect the tourism industry.

No female foreigner murdered the rich *farang* with durian juice. Preposterous! Obviously a local heard of the *farang's* fortune and murdered him for it. Or perhaps his unsavory gambling associates killed him."

Lily looked a bit irritated by her husband's certainty that the foreign woman wasn't the culprit. "Perhaps the woman followed him from America," Lily proposed. "A woman scorned, maybe. A stalker." She looked keenly at Cornelia in a way that made her nervous. Cornelia thought Lily was about to ask an uncomfortable question. *Are you the killer?*

"What would you like for dinner?" Lily asked.

"And that's not all," Ian continued. "I'm sure you know about the strangeness at the cloister."

"What strangeness?" Cornelia asked.

"Oh, you haven't heard about that?" Lily gasped.

Ian took over. "The cloistered nuns, every morning, walk out on the Cloister Walk on their way to morning mass," he explained. "They can't be exposed to, er, regular air, or something. Anyway, every morning, they walk out on their enclosed, elevated walkway, and beneath them a strange new—figure— has been carved from the shrubbery in the garden below. It's a-a topiary, it seems."

"But they don't know who's doing it," Lily breathed.

"What kind of figures?" Cornelia asked, bewildered. "You mean like—peacocks or something?"

"Nobody knows," Lily whispered. "The first figure which appeared from the shrubbery was a ship. Then came a ball. That's it. Just a ball! And then, the strangest of all—" here, Lily shuddered. "Two frightening-looking figures. One seems to be a man. The other, I think, a female. And their faces are similar, almost as if they are family. Father-daughter, maybe. Or brother-sister. Although it's hard to tell since they are carved from…shrubbery. They have a very eerie power."

"It's not just people carved from the shrubbery. It's words. And numbers," Ian reminded Lily. "Very peculiar."

"What words?" Cornelia asked.

"*Three Pet*," Ian said. "For the ball."

"Three Pet?"

"And for the ship, *Seven Gen*," Ian continued. "And for the two people, *Eleven Rev*. A code of some kind, I think."

"It's the work of ghosts," Lily declared firmly. "Spirits live in the trees. They are trying to come out—to emerge. They're unhappy about something. Trying to send a message to us."

"Nonsense," Ian said sharply. "Somebody's doing it. The only question is why? I'll lay you money it has something to do with that crazy Brother Lek. He's taken to calling himself One of Two Witnesses. Maybe he's carving himself and the other so-called *witness* out of the shrubbery to create a buzz. As a sort of marketing campaign. To get people to visit his weird little rock garden and spend money there." Ian's expression darkened. "It's dangerous business, calling too much attention to religion. If the uproar continues, the government will intervene. It will bring trouble to the Cloister."

"Have either of you ever seen Brother Lek?" Cornelia asked hopefully. "At least a picture of him?"

Ian frowned. "Well, no. He's a bit mysterious, that one."

"He's like a ghost himself," Lily remarked, a faraway look in her eyes.

Cornelia's head was beginning to throb. She had come to Laos to visit Brother Lek's sculptures and try to learn more about the mystery of the Two Witnesses and her own missing grandfather. And now the Two Witnesses were popping up in the nearby cloister's garden, carved from the shrubbery? It was a male and female, which Lily proposed might be father-daughter, or brother-sister. But what if it was husband-wife? Cornelia offered up a *yim mai awk* smile to Ian and Lily, the smile of someone who couldn't quite finish their smile through the pain. She said: "I think I need to go send some e-mails."

Lily inclined her head in the direction of the adjacent bookstore/internet café. "You know the way," she said. She looked down at Cornelia with a questioning expression on her face, taking note of Cornelia's stretched smile. "Are you O.K?" Then, without waiting for an answer, Lily declared: "You walked up from the riverbank instead of arriving of by *tuk-tuk*." It was a statement, not a question.

Cornelia swallowed hard and lied. "I arrived in Vientiane by *tuk-tuk* earlier today. I just wanted to go for a river ride this afternoon." Her voice sounded thin, her explanation lame.

"Smiling Cornelia," Lily said approvingly, beaming. She cocked her head and scrutinized Cornelia, her expression suddenly sober. "But your smile is so sad. No matter. You'll cheer up when you see Chanya."

"What?" Cornelia asked.

"Chanya," Lily repeated. "You came here to meet him, didn't you?"

"Is he staying here, too?" Cornelia asked.

Lily looked strangely at Cornelia. "Of course. He always stays here. Room 312. Didn't he tell you? He said he came for tonight's Dragon Festival. I thought that's why you came, too." Her eyes widened. "Don't you still work together? Are the two of you having trouble? Is that why you're acting so odd?"

"Is he here now?" Cornelia asked. She couldn't keep her heart cool right now, no matter how much her grandmother or all the Thais in Thailand chided her.

Lily frowned. "Now that you mention it, I haven't seen him since yesterday morning. He mentioned he wanted to go look at the topiary." Lily's eyes were bright with concern—or was it suspicion? "Doesn't he know you're here? Did the two of you have a falling out? Are you—*stalking* Chanya?"

CHAPTER 14

O SETH TO LAD OF KRIMIOV

Cornelia pushed herself up from the table.

"I'm not stalking Chanya," she mumbled weakly.

Lily was eyeing Cornelia curiously. "What do you want for dinner?"

Cornelia waved feebly as she walked away. "Just e-mail," she replied. "I'll be right back." Actually, she had no intention of checking her e-mail. She was headed straight for the topiary. She had to see the male-and-female topiary. And hopefully Chanya. A man and a woman as the Two Witnesses. A husband and wife? Her grandmother and grandfather? Lily thought it was a father and daughter. But if Brother Lek was one of the Witnesses... A strange sensation passed through Cornelia. Maybe it was a grandfather-and-granddaughter topiary. A ludicrous thought, which Cornelia instantly rejected. She took a deep breath and tried to come at it from a different angle. Ignore the idea that Brother Lek was one of the Two Witnesses. But consider the crazy idea that Brother Lek *was* Cornelia's grandfather. With traumatic amnesia, maybe he had carved his lost *wife and son* out of the shrubbery. A male and a female who looked alike: a *mother and son* as the Two Witnesses. Maybe his repressed memories were emerging.

But was something mystical at work as well? Was Brother Lek inadvertently revealing the identity of the Two Witnesses: Cornelia's own grandmother and Cornelia's father? Grandmother was *certainly* a witness of some kind. Had she realized at her death that she herself was one of the Two Witnesses? *Oh, Grace, we have been wrong. We have been blind.* Was this the secret that God finally revealed to her? Was it her own artwork that was her way of witnessing and warning? Cornelia's father was already dead by that time. Had he created some lost artwork that Cornelia hadn't yet discovered? Her father had no artistic inclinations that she was aware of. He'd been a gifted mechanic with a passion for Harley-Davidson motorcycles. He'd inherited his father's passion for powerful engines and his love of feeling the wind on his face on the open road. A mechanic. So he'd worked with his hands, was *very talented*, in fact, with his hands. But had he been inspired, in his spare time, to sculpt or carve or forge some fantastic vision out of rock or wood or metal or glass?

"Cornelia!"

Startled out of her reverie, Cornelia whirled around. A tall, elegant African-American stood in the bookstore doorway.

"Ralph!" Cornelia cried. "It's so good to see you."

"But why are you passing by?" Ralph chided gently. "And why are you in such a hurry? Are you headed to the Dragon Festival?" Heavenly incense wafted from Ralph's shop, and otherworldly music played inside, plucked delicately on strings. Ralph and his bookstore radiated serenity, expertly soothing harried, homesick travelers with yoga lessons, hot tea, and an internet connection to home. Since he was born and raised in New Orleans, he himself was very familiar with the jarring, transformative experience of leaving home, wandering into new country, and winding up lost on mysterious byways. "I want this to be a way station for travelers," Ralph had explained to Cornelia. "They have been looking outside of themselves for so many miles, stunned by strangeness, searching for their next exotic destination. Now I want them to stop, be still, and look *inside* themselves. I want them to ask: Where am I going? What am I looking for?"

Right now, Cornelia was looking for Chanya, Brother Lek, two stolen paintings from childhood, Two Witnesses, her long-lost grandfather, and peace of mind.

"Have you seen Chanya?" Cornelia blurted out. "I'm trying to find him."

Ralph frowned slightly. "No," he answered. "Where did he go?"

"I think he's at the topiary," Cornelia said. "He wanted to go look at the cloister topiary."

Ralph's mild gaze hardened. "*That* was a mistake," he said curtly.

"What do you mean?" Cornelia asked anxiously. "Why was it a mistake?"

Ralph looked around and lowered his voice, suddenly appearing un-serene and deeply paranoid. "Because something is wrong over there at the cloister. Day after day, those sisters follow the same routine. Every day for years they walk across that covered, elevated walkway, that—that Cloister Walk, to get to the church. So they never have to enter the world, they can remain cloistered. Suddenly strange figures start showing up in the shrubbery beneath the Cloister Walk. Instead of floating across on their private walkway, the sisters *stop*. They're shocked. They start talking and pointing. Calling others to come. Every morning it's a new figure. People are noticing. People like Chanya are coming to look. The Laotian government won't like a religious body stirring up trouble like that. Stirring people up with theories of the supernatural. Is it from God? Is it ghosts?"

"Well," Cornelia said. "Is it?"

Ralph barked out a short laugh. "Not God. Not ghosts. Certainly it's of human origin." He narrowed his eyes at Cornelia. "Perhaps Chanya believes in ghosts, being Thai and all. But don't tell me you believe that."

"But which humans are doing it, Ralph?" Cornelia asked desperately. "And why?"

Ralph looked around again carefully. "I don't think it's safe for us to be standing out here talking. Voices carry," he said softly. "Come inside for a moment."

Cornelia followed Ralph into the cool shop where a ceiling fan whirred gently overhead. On every side, books lined the walls, from classics like *Heart of Darkness* to Agatha Christie mysteries to books on yoga, meditation and travel. Near the door, a travelers' bulletin board displayed a variety of notices.

Seeking riverboat partner from Luang Prabang to Huayxay. Inquire at Mekong Guest House. Ask for Neil from Scotland.

Australian in Udon Thani Central Prison for drug offense seeks English-speaking visitors.

Beware Sop Hun/Tay Trang border crossing. Bribes required if crossing by motorbike.

"Let's sit for a moment," Ralph said, gesturing to a chair.

Cornelia plunked down in the chair. Ralph scrutinized her carefully.

"Your smile is strained," he said grimly. "Like a lid trying to contain a boiling pot. Why is this topiary of such great concern to you and Chanya?"

"The Two Witnesses," Cornelia mumbled. "Weren't they carved in the shrubbery?"

"It's a P.R. stunt," Ralph said dismissively. "Brother Lek is trying to attract more followers, or tourists, to his compound. That's what I think this is all about. He needs more followers and visitors, more *funds*, to keep it going."

"But I talked to an old monk who said Brother Lek's sculpture had a strange power," Cornelia argued.

Ralph hesitated. "Perhaps he was on the right path all those years ago. Perhaps he's lost his way, not unlike..." he trailed off.

"Kurtz?" Cornelia supplied.

Ralph smiled. "Let's hope he's not that far gone." He paused. "Although I do wonder why he chose the Cloister to pull his stunt. He knows as well as anyone that attracting the government's attention will only bring trouble. They could close down the Cloister, they could confiscate all his precious stone carvings. His *hallucinations*. They could arrest him. They could arrest innocent people, like the nuns." Ralph frowned and shook his head. "Why would he do that?"

Cornelia's heart was loud in her ears. "Unless, like you said, he's lost his way," she said quietly. "Have you ever seen Brother Lek? Even a picture of him?"

Ralph looked thoughtful. "Now that you mention it. No. Never. He is one slippery fish. But not long ago, one of his followers wandered in here. Dressed in white. Looking pasty white, too, I might add. *Do you have any texts about the Two Witnesses?* That's what she asked."

"What did you tell her?" Cornelia asked.

"I said, *Try the Bible.*" Ralph flashed a wry smile. "She must have been special. Trusted. I suspect Brother Lek was trying to bone up on his knowledge of the Two Witnesses to make sure he fit the bill."

Or maybe because he suspected he really was one of the Two Witnesses—or he knew who they were. Cornelia glanced around the shelves and toward the back of the shop where the computer sat. "What do you know about Seth? Or a place called Krimiov?"

Ralph looked sharply at Cornelia. "Krimiov sounds Russian, but I haven't a clue," he said. "But Seth—that's a subject I'm familiar with." He stood abruptly. "Let me pour you a cup of tea."

"You know about Seth?" Cornelia felt a surge of excitement. Maybe she would at last decode her grandmother's final, mysterious message, identifying the Two Witnesses.

"Seth was the third son of Adam," Ralph explained, his back to Cornelia as he poured and stirred. "You know, after Cain and

Abel. In fact, God supposedly gave Seth as a replacement after Abel was murdered."

Ralph set a cup of steaming jasmine tea in front of Cornelia. The delicious fragrance wafted through the bookstore and Cornelia felt herself relax—she hadn't even realized how tense she'd been.

"Cain and Abel," Cornelia repeated slowly. The twang of a sitar vibrated in the air, and Cornelia felt both soothed and hypnotized by the meditation music. Well, Cain and Abel were at least biblical, so maybe she was finally on the right track.

"Before Adam died, he supposedly shared profound secrets with Seth. Adam was the only man to walk with God in the garden, after all. So maybe he shared the secrets of God. One secret Adam revealed to Seth was that the world was destined to be destroyed twice—once by flood and once by fire. Seth reportedly recorded all cosmic knowledge on two pillars so that the information would be preserved during these apocalypses. There are rumors—even to this day—of the two pillars still existing. Maybe buried beneath the desert sands, or at the bottom of an ancient sea, or in the densest jungle."

Cornelia paused between sips of tea, picturing the crumbling pillars covered by choking vines. "What kind of cosmic knowledge did the pillars contain?"

"Astronomy, science, the like," Ralph suggested. "Maybe the secrets of our solar system, our universe, our beginnings, our end. The secrets of God. I don't know."

Cornelia frowned. Two pillars? Could they be connected to the Two Witnesses? Or was she desperately reaching? The two pillars, though mute, could be witnesses to the two apocalypses, with their inscriptions, their warnings. *Seth* was a witness, too. A witness to the coming apocalypses. A witness to sacred knowledge preserved through the apocalypses. A witness to the secrets of God.

"But that's not all," Ralph said. Cornelia shifted uneasily. "There was another Seth, a shadow Seth, if you will."

"A shadow Seth." Cornelia was alert, no longer lulled by the mystical music. A second Seth. *Two* Seths. Two Witnesses?

"Not a son of Adam. Not even human," Ralph said softly. "Seth, the god of chaos. The god of absolute evil."

Cornelia shivered. "Spooky stories you're telling me."

Ralph laughed. "Well, you asked."

A bell jingled as someone pushed the bookstore door open.

"A customer," Ralph said. "At last."

"What am I, chopped liver?" Cornelia asked.

"You are a friend," Ralph said. "But I must go to work. I need to sell a book or some internet minutes."

"Thanks for the tea," Cornelia said, rising. She paused, digging into her knapsack. "I know you said you'd never seen Brother Lek...but one time his follower came in here, looking for books." She held out the fifty-year-old photograph of her grandfather. "Maybe you could post this on the travelers' bulletin board for a little while? See if anyone recognizes this man? Maybe one of Brother Lek's followers will look at it? Or someone else who has seen Brother Lek?"

Ralph took the photograph from Cornelia, examining it carefully. "O.K. Is it Brother Lek?"

"That's the million-dollar question," Cornelia said. "And please be careful with it. I'll be back to pick it up again soon."

"Cornelia," Ralph said in a warning tone. "Don't go to the cloister. Don't get mixed up in that topiary business. Find Chanya and take him back to Bangkok. I'm telling you, this is serious. If the authorities become involved, it could lead to arrests. And believe me, you don't want to end up in a Lao prison."

"Thanks for the warning," Cornelia said, giving him her best *yim dor thaan* smile: *But I'm going to go ahead and do what I think is best anyway.*

CHAPTER 15

TROUBLE IN THE TOPIARY

The convent and its topiary garden were only a short walk away, down a dusty, rutted road. But even if Cornelia hadn't known where the topiary was, she couldn't have missed it. To her great surprise, the convent grounds and topiary were brightly lit by spotlights, and surrounded by crowds. Food cart vendors under umbrellas were lined up outside the convent wall, and gawkers had scrambled atop the wall in order to view the topiary grounds inside. Whole roasted fish and chicken sizzled alongside grilled snails and squid-on-a-stick. Families had spread out bamboo mats beneath coconut trees and appeared to be picnicking for the evening. One vendor was hawking white T-shirts, featuring the ragged topiary form of the Two Witnesses in black silhouette. Cornelia picked up one of the T-shirts and was disappointed that she couldn't make out much detail. Had she secretly been hoping that the male Witness would look like that old photograph of her grandfather? Had she expected to see the profile of a man leaning against a Jaguar convertible?

The T-shirt image resembled two humans, but Cornelia couldn't even ascertain gender. She fervently hoped the actual topiary sculpture would prove more revealing. Underneath the image was Laotian writing which Cornelia suspected said "Two Witnesses," or possibly *Eleven Rev.* What in the world did that stand for? Eleven Reverends? It might as well say Twelve Lords a Leaping. That's how helpful the enigmatic phrase was to Cornelia.

"Two thousand kip only," the vendor said in English, holding up a T-shirt.

Cornelia offered him a polite *yim thak thaai* smile and gestured toward the convent wall. "I want to see the real thing first," she explained.

"You buy T-shirt, I help you on wall," the vendor proposed. Cornelia judged the smooth stone wall to be about eight feet high, with no footholds. She was short, and someone would have to boost her up. It might as well be the T-shirt vendor.

"Will you take Thai baht?" she asked. Having entered the country illegally, she hadn't even had a chance to exchange currency yet. "And by the way, have you seen a Thai man named Chanya around here?"

The T-shirt vendor hadn't seen Chanya, but accepted the Thai currency. Cornelia stuffed the new T-shirt into her knapsack, and a few moments later, situated herself on the stone ledge above the topiary garden. She scanned the crowd, hoping she might see Chanya in the mix. The sun was sinking and the crowd, unlike the topiary garden, was not well-lit. Several floodlights had been erected on the walls, aimed directly into the garden below. A young Laotian man sat beside Cornelia, drinking Beer Lao.

"Have you seen a Thai man around here named Chanya?" Cornelia asked hopefully.

When the young man smiled at her helplessly, she repeated her question in Thai. The Laotian language was similar to the Thai dialect spoken across the river, and Cornelia hoped he would understand what she was saying.

"No," the young man replied in Laotian, still smiling courteously. "No Thai man."

Maybe, if Cornelia was lucky, Chanya would spot her up on the wall. In the meantime, she would power up her phone again and try to call him.

"I am waiting to see the spirit move," the Laotian said. He gestured toward the topiary. "I am waiting to see the spirit create. I want to see it!"

Cornelia smiled encouragingly, feeling guilty that she was on her phone while the man spoke so enthusiastically about the mystery in the topiary below. The background image which sprang to life on her phone was of Chanya teaching math to a group of boys in the slum. His face shone, possibly from perspiration, possibly from intense focus. Whatever task he was engaged in always absorbed him completely. When he was teaching children or organizing a game of slum *takraw*, his demeanor was patient and serene, as if he'd entered another dimension and left adult concerns behind. When the activity with the kids ended, Chanya always snapped back to reality, and began to frown and worry once again. Cornelia felt a stab of longing at seeing his face. His phone had gone immediately to voice mail, so Cornelia left a brief message that was sure to get his attention.

"I'm on the convent wall, looking at the topiary. I was hoping you'd be here. *Where are you?*"

Switching off the phone to preserve her dwindling battery, Cornelia re-focused her attention on the topiary garden below. A giant banyan tree, gnarled and twisted, crouched in the midst of the garden, its massive trunk encircled by multi-colored strips of satin, indicating a spirit dwelling therein. Nearby, three topiary figures had been skillfully sculpted from the shrubbery. The first shrubbery sculpture was clearly that of a boat. Cornelia could also see the words which Ian had mentioned, carved beside the boat: *Seven Gen.*

The next topiary figure was a large ball, just as Ian and Lily had said. But the ball wasn't perfectly spherical. It had rough, irregular patches scattered across it. Were they deliberate, or signs of limited skill? The words beside it read, *Three Pet.*

The final figure was what Cornelia had come for. She leaned forward as far as she dared to examine the Two Witnesses. Both figures appeared to be clad in robes, but the tall, broad-shouldered figure had shorter hair while the smaller, slighter figure had longer hair, which seemed to indicate a male and female. And the words: *Eleven Rev.* Cornelia tried to distinguish the facial features of the two figures—was it her father? Her grandfather? Her grandmother? *Herself?* Why did these crazy thoughts keep coming? She hadn't merely crossed a border separating Missouri from the Mekong, dividing the familiar from the strange. She had also crossed an invisible border into a troubling new dimension: A dimension in which a menacing apocalypse might or might not be coming, mysterious paintings and witnesses might or might not be warning, and it was increasingly difficult to separate fantasy from reality. The Apocalypse and the Witnesses couldn't possibly be real. Could they? It was crazy talk. Only it turned out it wasn't ditzy Miss Grace who was spewing the nonsense. *It was Cornelia's own grandmother.* And by following the trail of clues her grandmother had left behind, Cornelia was now likely wanted for murder, hiding without a visa in a land whose prisons were infamous. How had this happened? She wanted to disentangle herself and be back in the slum, sweating and teaching English in the morning heat, soaking up Thai spices in the evening with Chanya. Instead she was sitting on a wall looking down into a convent garden in Laos for signs of ghosts. The topiary was unevenly lit, a mixture of blinding light and impenetrable darkness. A gusting breeze set all the figures into occasional, unsettling motion—the boat appeared to rock dangerously, out of control, as if it might capsize. The Two Witnesses began to gesticulate wildly, as if they were warning...And the globe—the globe *turned.*

Cornelia realized the "ball" was definitely a globe. The earth? Were the irregular patches which jutted up here and there possibly mountains? Then there were the words carved beside each figure: *Seven Gen* beside the boat. Seven generations? The seventh generation? *Three Pet* beside the globe. That one was a puzzler. But *Eleven Rev...* Not Eleven Reverends. Eleven Revelations? A light went on in Cornelia's mind.

The young man to Cornelia's left nudged her, startling her. He seized her arm, steadying her.

"Sorry," he said. His face pale, he thrust a piece of paper into Cornelia's hand. "Read."

It appeared to be a flier of some sort, containing only two sentences. The two sentences were printed in Laotian, Thai, English, and French. They read:

The spirit in this garden is being frightened away by the bright lights and loud crowds. Please leave this place in peace so the spirit can come again.

"Who wrote this?" Cornelia asked, but the young man next to her had already jumped down and disappeared into the crowd.

"The nuns wrote it." Someone sitting on the other side of Cornelia spoke up. Whoever it was spoke Australian-accented English, but was sitting far enough away that Cornelia couldn't see him in the dark. "The nuns are handing out these fliers, trying to scare spectators away. The nuns are afraid of the government. It has nothing to do with frightened spirits." The disembodied voice was briefly silent. "At least, that's what I heard over at the guest house where I'm staying."

People were jumping down from the convent wall and scurrying away like rats abandoning a sinking ship. The floodlights on the wall abruptly shut off, plunging the convent garden below into darkness.

"Uh-oh. The police have arrived to break this party up. I think I'll vanish, too. Smoked something earlier I shouldn't have. Cheers."

Cornelia felt trapped like a deer in headlights. She might be able to slip past the Laotian police in the darkness and the crowd. But her blonde hair might also attract attention. What if they were searching for her? What if the Thai police had notified the Lao police? What if they asked to see her visa? Thinking about the trouble she was in left her momentarily dizzy. To be arrested for *murder*... The convent wall was almost deserted, now. Cornelia was one of the few still on it, and she was becoming more noticeable with each passing moment. Why hadn't she at least donned a hat before she left the guest house? It was time to make a decision. Cornelia took a deep breath, tightened her grip on her knapsack, and slipped off the wall into the inky depths of the topiary garden below.

CHAPTER 15

A SPIRIT IN THE NIGHT

Cornelia crouched in the darkness of the topiary garden, flattened against the convent wall. On the other side of the wall, a loudspeaker squawked police commands, while motorcycles revved and tuk-tuks sped off into the night. But on Cornelia's side of the wall, it was eerily silent. The only sound was the rustling of the topiary figures in the restless breeze. As her eyes adjusted to the darkness, Cornelia could make out the twisted banyan tree, limbs rattling in the wind, as well as the cloister walk which arched overhead. The cloister walk connected the convent on one end with a chapel on the other end. Cornelia saw no lights at all inside the convent, but she could detect a faint red glow coming from inside the chapel.

Gradually, the din on the other side of the wall subsided. Cornelia no longer heard the police loudspeaker nor any voices, and, thankfully, she detected nothing on her own side of the wall either. Relieved, she sank to the ground, her back against the convent wall, and unzipped her knapsack. She felt hidden by the darkness and shrubbery, but she prudently kept her phone inside the knapsack to hide its glow, checking to see if Chanya had responded to her message. He hadn't. An image of the anti-Christmas airport decor appeared on her phone. Denuded, beheaded trees littered the airport like the aftermath of a terrible storm. No comforting image of Chanya popped up this time. Nothing would have made Cornelia happier at this moment than to hear from him—to *see* him. To tell him everything. Cornelia was literally alone in the dark, and now that she was in the topiary itself, with no sign of Chanya, she wasn't sure what to do next. Or maybe she *was* sure. She needed to go to Brother Lek's garden of statues. Where else could Chanya be? She just didn't relish the prospect of venturing out again, a wanted woman. But she had to find him. Where was he? What had happened to him? She would return to her room at the guest house, pick up her sunglasses, and buy a ball cap. Ian and Lily sold *Mekong Guest House* ball caps and T-shirts to backpackers and tourists. With that rather flimsy disguise, she would set off for Brother Lek's dream of stone.

Cornelia was about to turn the phone off again, when she noticed the pocket Bible inside the knapsack. She remembered what had occurred to her while sitting on the wall just prior to the police raid. *Eleven Rev.* Not Eleven Revelations. *Revelation Eleven.* What exactly was in Revelation Chapter Eleven? By the light of her cell phone, Cornelia read:

And my two witnesses will prophesy for 1,260 days, clad in sackcloth. They are the two olive trees and the two candlesticks, and they stand before the Lord of the earth. If anyone attempts to attack them, fire erupts from their mouths and destroys their enemies. If anyone tries to injure them, that one will die in the same way. They are empowered to shut the heavens so that it doesn't rain while they are prophesying, and they are empowered to change the waters into blood and to smite the earth with plague as often as they want.

Now when they have completed their witnessing, the beast that comes up from the abyss will attack them and overpower and kill them. Their bodies will lie exposed in the great city—also known as Sodom and Egypt—where the Lord was crucified. For three and a half days inhabitants from every tribe, language and nation will look at their corpses and refuse to bury them. Those who dwell on earth will gloat and exchange gifts with glee, because these two prophets had tortured the consciences of those who dwell on earth.

But after three and a half days, the breath of God filled them, and they rose to their feet, and terror gripped those who saw them. Then they heard a voice from heaven cry out to them, "Come up here."And they went in a cloud up to heaven, while their enemies watched.

At that instant there was a terrible earthquake and a tenth of the city collapsed. Seven thousand people died in the earthquake, and those who were left were terrified and glorified the God of heaven.

It was the story of the Two Witnesses in the Book of Revelation— the same story Cornelia's grandmother had shared with Cornelia eighteen years earlier, at Miss Grace's urging. It was the same story Cornelia's grandmother had revealed through ominous scriptures and disturbing images in the painting, *Satanic Christmas*. The phrase *Eleven Rev* simply confirmed what Cornelia already suspected about the man and woman in the topiary: they were meant to be the Two Witnesses. Marcella had said the Two Witnesses were male—Moses and Elijah. Yet Revelation Chapter Eleven, Cornelia realized, did not specify which gender the Two Witnesses were. Whoever had carved these Two Witnesses—whether a Laotian tree spirit or a sly Brother Lek—had carved a male and a female. Why?

Excitedly, Cornelia flipped through the Bible to Genesis Chapter Seven. *Seven Gen.* It wasn't just a ship. It was *Noah's Ark.*

And the waters flooded the earth: and the highest mountains on earth were completely covered.

And all creatures that breathed and lived on land, died.

And only Noah survived, and those that were with him in the ark.

And what about the mysterious *Three Pet*? There was a book called Peter, wasn't there? Cornelia checked the Bible's table of contents. First Peter. Second Peter. But no Third Peter. Still, First Peter had a Chapter Three.

The chapter covered a range of subjects, declaring inner beauty more important than outer beauty, insisting on repaying evil with love, and—here it was. Another mention of Noah escaping destruction through the Ark. But what did that have to do with the globe carved so cleverly that it looked like it was spinning? Were the rough, jutting patches across the globe crashing waves, threatening to swallow all the land? Is that why the globe was accompanied by a scripture mentioning Noah's Ark?

Cornelia turned to Second Peter, intrigued to see that it also had a chapter three. She started to read. That was when she saw a ghostly figure gliding through the garden.

Cornelia held her breath and watched as the ghost moved silently toward the topiary. Where had it come from—inside the tree? Was it Brother Lek? It was impossible to see the figure clearly in the darkness, but it was slight, and shrouded in white. Its back to Cornelia, it turned abruptly and its eyes flared momentarily in the night before going dark, like a beacon in a lighthouse. Cornelia watched as a flash of light then sprang from the figure's hands, like fire. Ghostly fire? A fire-breathing Witness? Cornelia wanted to melt into the wall, or vault over it and escape. Could she make herself invisible just by wishing? It suddenly seemed extremely stupid to be chasing after the Two Witnesses from the Book of Revelation. Witnesses who could breathe fire to destroy their foes. The ghost floated closer, but now Cornelia recognized the fiery gleam in its hands—it was the flash of a blade. Spirit or not, it appeared to be using ordinary hedge clippers to do its deed.

And the deed was not creative—it was pure destruction. The ghost was destroying Noah's Ark, hacking it with garden shears, sinking it. Cornelia watched in stunned disbelief as the ghost made short work of the ship and turned to the globe, slashing it in half. Her hand shaking, Cornelia slowly snaked her phone out of her knapsack. She held it up carefully and aimed. As soon as she pressed "record," the phone made a distinct *click*. The ghost froze in mid-clip.

"Chanya?"

Such a dear, familiar name whispered in the topiary darkness shocked Cornelia. Who was this vengeful spirit, obliterating the elaborately carved mystery figures, and at the same time calling for Chanya? Trembling, Cornelia rose to her feet as the spirit inched closer.

"Chanya, is that you?" the spirit asked again. "I'm so—"

"I'm not Chanya," Cornelia admitted to the ghost. "But I'm his friend. Who are you?"

Cornelia found herself face-to-face with a diminutive nun, dressed in a white dress and habit, whose large gray eyes blinked owlishly through thick eyeglasses.

"Oh, dear," the nun whispered. "Are you his English teacher, Cornelia?"

The nun's name was Sister Pen. An English-speaking Thai nun on missionary assignment in Laos, she led Cornelia to the back row of the chapel where they both now huddled in darkness. In the front of the chapel, a flame trembled inside a red glass candle holder, which hung suspended above a gleaming brass tabernacle used to house the Blessed Sacrament. The candle was reflected in Sister Pen's thick lenses, where twin flames danced feverishly.

"Oh, dear," Sister Pen repeated. "Whatever brought you here? Never mind. Don't tell me. I know. You are looking for Chanya."

"Yes," Cornelia agreed. "Yes, I am. Why did you think I was Chanya? Have you seen him?"

"Of course, of course," Sister Pen said. "He was here just yesterday. I've known Chanya for so many years. I served in the slum when he lived there, as a boy. Where his English teachers now work. I have invited Chanya to bring English teachers here, too."

Chanya had lived in the slum as a boy? Why hadn't he ever mentioned this to Cornelia? It explained a lot. His sorrowful passion, his unflagging dedication, his complete and utter inability to separate himself from his work. Yet for the first time, Cornelia also saw the stoic side of Chanya, the cool-hearted Chanya—who had never mentioned that he himself had come from the slums.

"But why was Chanya here yesterday?" Cornelia asked. She knew he was chasing down stolen paintings and hunting for missing witnesses. What she really wanted to know was what he had told Sister Pen. Sister Pen had seen him much more recently than Cornelia herself had. She had the most current information.

"Oh, dear, oh, dear," Sister Pen whispered mournfully. "I'm afraid it's all my fault. You see, Chanya came here to examine the Two Witnesses Topiary."

"Yes," Cornelia agreed. "And what did he say when he was here? Where has he gone now?"

Sister Pen turned and regarded Cornelia through her thick lenses, which no longer reflected the candlelight. "You seem unsurprised by this news," she whispered. "About the Two Witnesses."

"Yes," Cornelia said. "I *am* unsurprised. I mean—I knew he was looking into Brother Lek being one of the Two Witnesses. And after I arrived in Laos, I also heard about the Two Witnesses Topiary. So it seemed likely Chanya would come here. Maybe Brother Lek is behind these creations? To draw attention to his sculptures? To drum up business?"

Sister Pen looked away and twisted her hands fretfully. "No," she said quietly. "Brother Lek is not behind this topiary. I'm afraid I am."

Cornelia was too surprised to speak, but it didn't matter. As if in need of confession, Sister Pen poured out her story.

"Many years ago, before I became a nun, I was a disciple of Brother Lek. Yes, I was his follower. I followed him all the way to the banks of the Mekong River. I was the creator behind so many of his sculptures." She bit her lip. "The early ones. The first ones."

"You mean—Brother Lek wasn't the sculptor?" Cornelia asked, shocked.

A tiny laugh escaped from Sister Pen. "Of course not. No, he had no gift in his hands. He had no inner sight. Me, I had no outer sight. My eyesight was so weak. So I used my hands to express what I saw inside myself. Brother Lek's gift was with people. Something I lacked utterly. His charisma drew lost souls like a magnet." The tiny nun sighed. "I was just such a soul. I know you can't imagine it, seeing me now. But when I was young, I was—" Sister Pen hesitated. "I was deeply drawn to Brother Lek. And he to me."

A romance gone awry? "Brother Lek is an American, isn't he?" Cornelia asked cautiously.

"Of course," Sister Pen said.

"Was he an American soldier? From the Vietnam War? Before he became a Buddhist monk, I mean. Before he became Brother Lek." Finally, Cornelia had found someone who had actually seen Brother Lek when he was young, but she'd left the photograph of her grandfather behind in Ralph's bookstore. But she could come back with the picture, later, and show it to Sister Pen. She *would* come back.

"A soldier from the Vietnam War? Brother Lek?" Sister Pen frowned. "If he was, he never told me. But he was secretive. He had left his past behind, he always said. He didn't wish to resurrect it. He had shaved his head and entered a Buddhist monastery. But then he left and started—a cult, really. And I followed."

"So what happened next?" Cornelia asked apprehensively.

Sister Pen gestured dismissively. "I eventually came to my senses. My father came and rescued me from the cult. But my sculptures have endured. So many young souls pilgrimage here, seeking them out. They hear of them, they come to see them, fascinated, intrigued. They see them as portals into—another world. And so they are. But it's not their world. It's not a safe world."

Cornelia's scalp prickled.

"And of course other sculptures have been added since mine. Darker creations. Twisted. Violent." Sister Pen gazed, unseeing, past Cornelia. "They are venturing further and further into a dangerous spirit world. A world from which they might never return. My sculptures have drawn many searching souls into Brother Lek's charismatic chains." Sister Pen straightened, her voice firm. "Yes, he enslaves them. I was trying to—to counter his charm. I was trying to create sculptures that drew people away from his false Witness, toward the true Witnesses. I was trying to undo the damage I'd done," Sister Pen said. "It was penance, I suppose. I asked permission for night vigils in the chapel. On the nights when I was praying in the chapel, I would slip outside and create a topiary, along with an accompanying scripture."

"Noah's Ark," Cornelia said. "Genesis Seven."

Sister Pen smiled, looking faintly pleased.

"And then First Peter 3," Cornelia continued. "Noah's Ark again. The world covered in water."

"Oh, no," Sister Pen objected. "Not First Peter Three. Second Peter Three. *By water, the ancient world was covered and destroyed. By the same word, the present heavens and earth are destined for fire...*Once by water. Once by fire. *The Day of the Lord,*" Sister Pen whispered in the hushed chapel.

"So those weren't waves of water crashing over the earth," Cornelia breathed. "It was a tsunami, all right. Of fire." And wasn't that what Ralph had told her about the missing Twin Pillars of Seth? Two apocalypses—one by water. The second by fire. Two pillars to preserve knowledge. Two Witnesses. And two paintings.

The red candle flickered in the deep stillness. It felt as if someone, or something, else was present. Cornelia strained to listen, but could hear only Sister Pen's labored breathing.

"But you see," Sister Pen said sadly. "I was too successful. The topiary began to draw crowds, and attract so much attention. People thought it was spirits at work. It became dangerous for the convent. The government was taking notice. So I had to stop it. That's what I was doing tonight. And I'd hoped Chanya had come back from his excursion to Brother Lek. I'd hoped he had realized Brother Lek was not a Witness, that he was a fraud."

"But you told him," Cornelia said. "Just like you told me. You told him that *you* were creating the topiary figures. Not Brother Lek."

Sister Pen hung her head. "I was too ashamed to tell him what I'd done. That I was the original sculpture creator, that I was the topiary garden sculptor. Chanya knows me only as the simple nun who brought rice and cooking oil to his mother, who helped him and his sisters when they were being beaten by his drug-addicted father. I can confess to you. You don't know me. You have never loved me, respected me, *needed* me. But I wasn't able to tell Chanya about my foolish past. Nor about my deceptive present which has now spun out of control. That's why I was desperately hoping he had come back. I *wanted* him to see what I was doing, destroying the topiary garden. I wanted to tell him the truth."

"So Chanya went to the sculpture garden, still thinking maybe Brother Lek had created the topiary," Cornelia said slowly. "Wondering if Brother Lek might be one of the Two Witnesses, as he claims." But surely Chanya hadn't been fooled. And yet—hadn't Cornelia herself wondered the very same thing? Cornelia rose to her feet in the darkened chapel. "I should go find Chanya."

"Of course, you must," Sister Pen agreed. She grabbed Cornelia's arm. "But be careful. Brother Lek is sly as a snake. Beware of his smile. If you see it—*yim mee lessanai*—you must *go*."

Yim mee lessanai. A smile which hides malice. A smile which means harm. Could the sinister Brother Lek be Cornelia's own grandfather? A man traumatized by war, whose memory was wiped away? A man who had died to his past and re-fashioned himself into something alien and new?

Yim mee lessanai. A smile which masks evil intent. Speaking of masks gave Cornelia an idea. "Sister Pen, I wonder if you can help me with something. So that I can reach Chanya safely."

A short time later, Cornelia prepared to step out into the night, dressed in the simple white habit of a nun.

"Thank you so much for your help," she whispered to Sister Pen.

"Anything to help Chanya," Sister Pen replied. She squeezed Cornelia's hand. "And you."

"Sister Pen, you said you wanted to reveal the True Witnesses instead of Brother Lek's false witness," Cornelia said.

"Yes, of course I did," Sister Pen said.

"But who *are* the Two Witnesses?" Cornelia asked. "Do you know?"

"Well, it was Father Bill who led me to understand," Sister Pen said. "He was the one who showed me—"

A door creaked behind Sister Pen and footsteps approached. Sister Pen pushed Cornelia out the door.

"One of the sisters is coming. Take a tuk-tuk and go."

CHAPTER 16
GARDEN OF GHOSTS

Cornelia stood in the shadow of towering gates and tugged at a dangling rope. Inside, a ponderous bell tolled. Cornelia strained to hear footsteps in response to the massive doorbell, but all she heard was silence.

Visiting hours were over, of course, and tours had ended for the day. It was too late to pose as a clueless tourist at the Garden of Ghosts, so it was convenient that Cornelia was dressed as a nun. *Garden of Ghosts.* Cornelia found the sculpture park's official name to be more than a little eerie. The courtyard just inside the iron gates lay shrouded in darkness. Coconut and banana trees stirred slightly, but the evening breeze had for the most part died. Sweat trickled down Cornelia's back.

She had briefly considered trying to sneak in, but the ten-foot walls and gates were effective in keeping someone as unprepared as Cornelia out. If she'd brought a ladder, or possessed enough rope and skill to scale the stone walls, she would have gone over in an instant. But realistically, she either had to wait until morning and arrive as a tourist, or ring the sonorous bell and hope that someone answered.

Someone finally did.

A ghostly figure floated toward the gate, wrapped bony fingers around the iron gate and peered out at Cornelia. Cornelia felt a prickle of unease although she could see it was merely a gaunt young Caucasian woman dressed in white. The young woman's pale green eyes widened slightly when she saw the small nun at the gate. When the young woman opened her mouth, it became apparent that she was French.

"I'm sorry, sister, but we are closed," she whispered. Her white hair was parted in the middle and fell like a curtain on either side of her face, giving the anemic girl an almost albino look. "We open to visitors tomorrow at 11 o'clock."

"I must see Chanya immediately," Cornelia said briskly. "I work with him in the slum. Please tell him Sister Cornelia is here. He is expecting me."

"There is no Brother Chanya here," the French girl replied. "And we are closed to visitors until tomorrow morning."

Belatedly, it occurred to Cornelia that Chanya may have taken a fake name. After all, *Satanic Christmas* had been stolen from him. He could hardly come here under his own identity. On the other hand, it was possible Chanya had already come and gone, posing as a tourist. Cornelia didn't want to think about the final option— that Chanya was being held here against his will. "Oh, of course," Cornelia bluffed. "Chanya wanted to choose a new name before he entered." At this point, she was desperate and would try anything to gain entrance. "He wanted to join you, but he wanted a new name for his, er, fresh start."

"You must mean John," the gatekeeper suggested. "Our newest novice. Brother John from Chiang Mai. He is Thai, but he chose the English name John for his new name."

"That must be him," Cornelia agreed recklessly. She hadn't the slightest idea if Chanya was posing as John. Chanya was from Bangkok, not Chiang Mai, but that could have been part of his disguise. "It's imperative that I see John right away. It's an emergency.

As I told you, I work with Brother John in the slum in, um, Chiang Mai. There is a great emergency there. Tell him that Sister Cornelia must speak with him immediately."

"Brother John cannot speak with you," the French girl repeated in a hushed tone. "He has taken a vow of silence for thirty days."

Cornelia was momentarily speechless herself. "Why?" she demanded abruptly.

The French girl gave a wan smile, her cheeks still bloodless. "He has joined our order. He must immerse himself in complete silence for the first thirty days. That is the requirement for any novice. After that, he may not communicate with any former acquaintances or outside contacts for one year. Only after Brother John has completed his novice training can he once again make contact with those from his..." This speech seemed to require enormous effort, and the girl's frail voice trailed off incomprehensibly.

Cornelia tried to hide her dismay. Chanya had fallen for the charismatic Brother Lek. So easily! So soon. He had to be brainwashed. Why else would Chanya have stayed and joined? Unless—was he being held against his will? This possibility filled Cornelia with panic.

Then Cornelia heard her grandmother's voice in her ear. "*Smile.*" A *yim cheun chom* smile rose instantly to Cornelia's lips: *I admire you.* "Yes, I am so proud of Brother John for deciding to take this step. How impressive it is here." Cornelia's smile deepened to include the spectral gatekeeper in this sweeping compliment. "And of course I know he isn't free to leave. That's why I'm here. He asked me to bring the funds."

The French porter furrowed her snow-white brow. "Funds?"

"Yes, Brother John wishes to make a sizable contribution, of course," Cornelia murmured. "He contacted me just before he started his silence and asked me to bring the donation with me."

"Oh!" the young woman breathed. "It's what we've been pray-ing for. To create a great sculpture of the Two Witnesses. A *giant* sculpture, Brother Lek says. Like the giant Buddha. People will come from everywhere to stand in its shadow. Oh, how generous of Brother John. We all felt the Two Witnesses in the topiary were a sign. That the Second Witness was near, that completion was upon us. How kind of you to travel all this way. I will certainly deliver the donation safely to Brother Lek. Perhaps you would like to phone tomorrow morning to make sure that your donation was safely...?" Again her voice faded before she could finish her thought.

"Brother John insisted that I *personally* hand the donation to Brother Lek," Cornelia said smoothly. "It's a significant amount. Surely you understand and don't take offense."

The pallid sentry hesitated, conflicted. "If it were daytime, it would be no problem. But to disturb Brother Lek after dark...He retires with the sun. He rises with the sun, as well."

"I have traveled all this way and have nowhere to sleep tonight. I am carrying a significant amount of money which leaves me feel-ing rather anxious and vulnerable. If something were to happen to me tonight, to the funds..." Her own voice trailed off, leaving the young French woman to imagine trying to explain to Brother Lek why she had turned away a nun who was bearing gifts which would enable the construction of the monument to the Two Witnesses. "Perhaps I could sleep here tonight and deposit the funds with Brother Lek first thing in the morning."

The wraithlike doorkeeper appeared to brighten slightly, nod-ding assent to this plan. Delicate spots of color briefly touched her cheeks. "My name, by the way, is Lorraine," she whispered as she unlocked the gate. The heavy gate groaned loudly in the silent night, making Cornelia wince. She hoped no one would come run-ning to investigate. Her plan was going smoothly and she didn't want further complication. Cornelia noticed that Lorraine, oddly enough, was barefoot.

"Yes, I'm sure we can find a bed for you tonight, and I'm sure Brother Lek will be thrilled to meet with you first thing in the morning."

Lorraine led the way, gliding silently, apparently satisfied that she had secured the sacred donation without disturbing Brother Lek after he'd retired for the night. Since Cornelia had no actual gift to give, she was grateful to have the entire night to find Chanya and investigate the Garden of Ghosts before her bluff was called. Of course, she also wanted to see Brother Lek, but that would have to wait until morning. Cornelia would worry later about the logistics of meeting Brother Lek and escaping from the Garden before they realized she had no "funds" to give. Then an odd thought occurred to her: If Brother Lek *was* her grandfather, would Cornelia even want to "escape?" A nearby dookay lizard clucked out its low, mournful call. Cornelia watched Lorraine's ethereal figure drift ahead of her. The scent of night-blooming jasmine wafted on the night air.

"What is Brother Lek like?" Cornelia asked.

Lorraine seemed startled by the question. She paused almost imperceptibly before resuming her ghostly glide. "He is one of Two Witnesses," Lorraine intoned. Her voice grew fainter. "When the Second Witness comes, then the sanctuary opens..." Lorraine sighed, her vocal chords exhausted.

To Cornelia, it sounded like a cult mantra. She'd been hoping for a spontaneous, enthusiastic response from Lorraine. Despite Sister Pen's warning, Cornelia didn't want to believe the worst about a man who might be her own grandfather. Maybe Brother Lek wasn't a corrupt cult leader. Maybe he was, at worst, confused. At best, maybe he was wise, benevolent and loved. Maybe he helped lost young people like poor Lorraine find direction in life. She obviously needed it. Besides, Sister Pen had history with Brother Lek. *Romantic* history. Maybe she'd fled to the convent to heal from a broken heart. She had been a troubled, guilt-ridden young soul, by her own admission. No wonder she couldn't be objective about Brother Lek. And look at her now! Creating and then destroying crazy sculptures in the middle of the night. She wasn't stable, even now. Sister Pen began to take on a vaguely sinister shape in Cornelia's mind. Maybe she had even been *manipulating* Cornelia.

There was something else about Sister Pen which made Cornelia uneasy. Sister Pen had said Brother Lek was no artist at all—that she herself had been the prodigy behind the mysterious stone creations. Until then, Cornelia had actually been entertaining the novel idea that her own grandfather was a visionary artist, like his wife, Cornelia's grandmother. This had led to an even more outrageous possibility—that her own grandparents had been the Two Witnesses. Was this what Grandmother had discovered at the end of her life, as she finally finished *Satanic Christmas*? Was this what had upset her so?

And yet, if Sister Pen was telling the truth, Brother Lek was no visionary artist at all. Scam artist was more like it. Unless...If her grandfather had lost his memory after the helicopter crash, fragments of his shattered past might still surface in unpredictable ways. Maybe he'd re-invented himself as a great visionary artist because of some buried memory of his lost wife.

"Does Brother Lek ever talk about his past life in the United States?" Cornelia probed. "I heard he was from Missouri, originally...although maybe I'm wrong."

"Missouri?" Lorraine repeated, sounding confused. "I— Brother Lek is the first of Two Witnesses..." Lorraine's thin voice sputtered briefly, then suddenly revived with a question of her own. "What was the emergency?"

"Emergency?"

"You said there was a great emergency in the slum program," Lorraine reminded her. They had reached a long, low building and paused outside a wooden door.

"Oh! Of course. Yes, some plumbing issues in the orphanage dormitory," Cornelia lied. "I need permission from Brother John to withdraw some funds for that repair. I hadn't expected him to take his vow of silence so *quickly*."

"Well, we can work something out," Lorraine whispered in a conspiratorial tone. "For large donors, there are usually..." Her voice dwindled. "I'm sure you could write a note for Brother John to read. That wouldn't violate his vow of silence."

"That's an excellent idea!" Cornelia said enthusiastically. "Is it possible you can hand the note to Chanya—I mean, Brother John—tonight?"

Lorraine considered. "I don't see why not," she decided. Obviously, disturbing a novice like Chanya after dark was not the grave offense that upsetting Brother Lek would be. As if to explain, Lorraine murmured, "Brother John is not sleeping. As a novice, Brother John has been given a special assignment. Every novice must prove himself, or herself, worthy to stay, by sculpting a new addition to our spectacle of stone. It's a test." Even more softly, Lorraine continued. "First, Brother John must meditate among the ghosts until he receives Brother Lek's image. All the sculptures spring from the mind of Brother Lek. All the sculptures spring from the Divine Well which flows from Brother Lek. Once Brother Lek and Brother John's minds meld, Brother John will begin to..." Lorraine's strength ran out. She pushed open the wooden door with a slight creak. "This is the women's quarters." she murmured. "There's an empty hammock here on the end that you may take. But first, why don't you write your note to Brother John, and I will deliver it to him right away."

Dear Brother John,

I have arrived with your generous donation which I will personally hand to Brother Lek tomorrow. I also need your written permission to withdraw funds to repair the recurring plumbing issue

*in the girls' dorm. Sister Lorraine has been so kind as to offer me
a hammock in the women's wing tonight. I know you have taken a
vow of silence, but I anxiously await your response.*
Faithfully,
Sister Cornelia

Cornelia folded the note demurely and handed it to Lorraine.
The message was innocuous enough to raise no alarms, Cornelia
thought—except of course with Chanya. He would no doubt be
very alarmed—unless he was under Brother Lek's sinister spell.
The door creaked again as Cornelia slipped obediently into the
women's wing, but she was careful to keep it slightly ajar. In the
faint light, she could see several long rows of hammocks suspended from the ceiling. Many of the hammocks were heavy with dark
shapes, and gauzy mosquito netting flowed over each one, giving
it the appearance of a chrysalis incubating new life. Apparently,
the disciples retired with the sun, as well. Cornelia peered through
the crack in the door and watched the unearthly Lorraine float
off into the darkness. Cornelia knew she couldn't possibly wait for
Chanya to come to her. What if Lorraine didn't deliver the note
after all? What if Chanya was actually imprisoned? Cornelia could
try to text Chanya again, but he hadn't replied in ages. Maybe he'd
relinquished his phone during his thirty days of silence. Maybe
the battery had died. Worse—maybe he was being held against
his will and his phone had been seized. Someone stirred in one of
the nearby hammocks, like a pupa struggling to emerge from its
cocoon. Cornelia winced as she pushed open the creaking door
one last time, but she had no choice but to slip back outside. She
couldn't lose sight of Lorraine.

After leaving the women's dorm, Lorraine moved swiftly past
the men's wing, as well as several other anonymous one-story
wooden structures, all completely dark. Maybe they were studios
where the actual sculpting was done. A kitchen or cafeteria? What

facilities did a cult need? What happened to cult members who mis-
behaved? Was there a jail? Ahead, Cornelia saw a building bathed
in the harsh glare of floodlights. Cornelia had to carefully skirt
the building and stick to the shadows because on all four sides
stood two guards each—eight in all. Each set of guards consisted
of a marble statue of a standing, roaring lion, and next to the lion,
a living, breathing human being. On all four sides, a flickering
torch was planted between the lion and the man. The four human
guards, instead of being draped in wispy white like Lorraine or
marble majesty like the lions, were bedecked in menacing cam-
ouflage and military helmets and carrying what appeared to be
black machine guns strapped across their chests. The building itself resembled a temple. A marble portico ran all the way around,
supported by blood-red columns around which emerald green
serpents wrapped themselves like ivy. The glazed red tile roof, ac-
cented with ornate gold flourishes, curved sharply upward to send
evil spirits flying. In jarring contrast, the exterior walls themselves
were plastered on two sides by giant posters, like a boarded up
building in a decaying inner city. On every poster was the color
photograph of one man. The man's giant face was white and bald.
His eyes were closed, as if he was asleep—or maybe dead. The
only trace of hair on the giant face was the pencil-thin eyebrows.
The nose was long, the lips thin and pale. It must be Brother Lek.
The face looked nothing like Cornelia's precious photograph of a
young, brown-haired American from fifty years ago. But what if he
had hair, what if he was fifty years younger? Was this a temple to
Brother Lek? Was it his living quarters? Whatever was inside was
certainly well-protected by the armed guards. And why were only
two walls decorated with Brother Lek's face? The other two walls
of the building were blank and white.

Cornelia felt relieved once she had passed the brightly lit temple and re-entered the darkness, but her relief didn't last long.
Up ahead, the white-robed Lorraine moved noiselessly among

scattered, incandescent figures. Unlike Lorraine, the softly glowing figures remained immobile. Were they novices like Chanya, meditating through the night to prove themselves? If Cornelia didn't know better, she would have thought the grounds were illuminated by ghosts, but Lorraine weaved her way smoothly through the sprinkled lights without missing a beat. As Cornelia neared one of them, it became apparent that the shimmering "spirit" was solid as rock. In fact, it *was* a rock. Cornelia had followed Lorraine straight into the heart of the Garden of Ghosts, where the sculptures, up close, no longer appeared ethereal, but decidedly earthly, resembling tombstones, or bones, gleaming in the moonlight. Cornelia moved near one of them, which she realized with horror was a pack of hyena-like creatures encircling a wounded pony which had fallen to one knee. The next sculpture was a massive snake, its body stretching into the distance, its jaws unhinged and its razor-sharp fangs dripping venom. No, it was only silver bells which dangled from the fangs and jingled eerily in the wind. Just outside the gaping jaws lay a wounded stone bird. Cornelia shuddered. Brother Lek's "stone dream" was more like a stone nightmare. Were all the sculptures of predators and prey? Were the disturbing images the product of a soldier's psyche, damaged by war? But Sister Pen had claimed *she* was the original source of these nightmarish sculptures. Cornelia felt another stirring of unease about Sister Pen.

Lorraine came to an abrupt stop causing Cornelia to momentarily panic before ducking inside the snake's giant mouth. Cornelia saw that the snake's body was hollow, creating a long tunnel which stretched behind her. Outside, Cornelia could see a sculpture of a man sitting cross-legged in meditation beneath a large cobra head, the cobra's hood fanned out to provide shelter. The man began to move, unsculpture-like, although the cobra head remained frozen. Dressed in a predictable white tunic, the man rose to his feet and turned and faced Lorraine. It was too dark to make out his face or to detect much else beneath his roomy clothing. Was it Chanya? Brother Lek? Maybe another night watchman, like the ghostly Sister Lorraine? Cornelia strained to hear Lorraine's muted mutterings. She tensed when Lorraine handed the note to the man in white. The man stared at the note for several moments, then crushed it in his palm. He looked around in the darkness.

"Sister Lorraine, I must be taken to Brother Lek immediately," Chanya thundered in the dark stillness. Cornelia wanted to cry at hearing his deep, hearty voice, wanted to reach out and grab him by his white sleeve. He still *sounded* like the good, old Chanya that Cornelia knew. But now that he knew that Cornelia was here, why did he want to see Brother Lek instead? Cornelia had been ready to step out of the snake's mouth and reveal herself as soon as Lorraine went away, although Chanya couldn't know that. He had no idea where Cornelia was. Still—why betray her to Brother Lek right away? What if Chanya were truly brainwashed? Cornelia hadn't known that Chanya had come from the trauma and chaos of the slum. He wore his hot heart on his sleeve, wept easily, and drank too much. Cornelia had abandoned him and gone home to America. He was vulnerable. Maybe too vulnerable to withstand someone who offered to solve every problem and make all pain go away. Isn't that what cults promised?

Lorraine murmured. "Brother John, you know...can't be disturbed..."

"Sister Lorraine, you don't understand. My meditation is finished. I have melded minds with Brother Lek. His dream has become mine. I know what Brother Lek wishes me to sculpt. *I have received my vision.*"

CHAPTER 17

THE FIRST WITNESS

Chanya's declaration triggered a flurry of activity. Any hopes Cornelia had of revealing herself to Chanya evaporated. Instead, Lorraine led Chanya straight to the brightly lit temple, where she had an urgent conversation with one of the guards. The guard entered the temple while another guard began to beat a drum. The drumming was obviously a summons because men and women, barefoot and dressed in white, began to pour out of the dormitories and gather round the temple. Cornelia pulled the nun's veil off her head. She was already wearing the simple white dress from Sister Pen, so maybe she could blend in. To be on the safe side, she kept her distance from both the crowd and the temple lights, taking refuge behind a leafy banana tree.

The drumming abruptly ceased and the temple floodlights went out. All the disciples in white whispered and stirred in the darkness, like a gathering of ghosts. Then a single spotlight sprang to life. Bathed in radiance stood a slight, bald man dressed entirely in black. Unlike his followers, Brother Lek wore no robes—only a black shirt, black pants, black shoes and black sunglasses. Then he spoke.

"Who has called us here?"

Chanya stepped forward and a second, smaller spotlight fell on him. "Brother John has."

"Brother John. What is your reason for waking us from our pleasant dreams, for dragging us into the blinding light?"

"Dear Brother Lek, I have received my vision. What you sent to me, I have received."

Cornelia was impressed by Chanya's confident, booming response, but also a little frightened. Chanya was either an excellent actor or had gone completely round the bend.

Brother Lek spoke again. "Brother John, what did you see? What have I given you? What has the Divine Well inside me brought forth? What vision will you bring to life in our garden of stone?"

"This night I have been haunted...*by two faces.* I have seen their faces in my dreams. I have heard their conversations," Chanya pronounced. "Brother Lek, you have truly blessed me. I am anointed by you. I know who the Two Witnesses are, and not only that. Now I am going to reveal them."

The crowd erupted. Chanya continued his speech above the furor.

"You, dear Brother Lek, are the First Witness," Chanya declared. "I have seen it for myself." The crowd cheered. "But I have even more miraculous news. *The Second Witness has arrived.*"

The crowd began to turn and look all around. Cornelia remained behind the banana tree.

"Who is it?" a man cried.

"Where is the Witness?" called someone else.

Brother Lek stood, black and immobile, in the light. He was too far away for Cornelia to see the expression on his face.

"I only know what I saw in my dream," Chanya continued. "My dream from Brother Lek. A stranger is among us. That stranger is the Second Witness."

Out of nowhere, Lorraine rushed into Chanya's spotlight. Cornelia noticed that pallid Lorraine had turned positively pink. And for the first time, Cornelia could hear every single word she said.

"I know who it is! The sister! She arrived here mysteriously tonight with a great gift. With the money, we can build the statue! The great statue of the Two Witnesses!" Lorraine paused, gasping for breath. "I knew the sister had brought a gift. But I did not know she also *was* the gift!"

Brother Lek spoke sharply. "What sister?" His gaze roamed over the crowd, his eyes unreadable behind his dark glasses.

"We all know what Brother Lek himself has declared," Chanya continued. "Only the Second Witness can enter into Brother Lek's sanctuary." Chanya gestured to Brother Lek's temple, with two walls displaying Brother Lek's giant face, and two walls completely blank. "*This* is the sanctuary of the Two Witnesses. One wall for Brother Lek. One wall for the Other Witness."

"One wall for Brother Lek," the crowd chanted. "One wall for the Other Witness."

"We have waited so long for the second face to appear on the temple walls!" Sister Lorraine cried.

Chanya turned and faced the dark woods beyond the light. "The Inner Sanctum is reserved for only the Two Most Worthy. Brother Lek is Number One. Sister Cornelia, Second Witness, come forward into the light."

CHAPTER 18

THE SECOND WITNESS

Cornelia had no intention of emerging from the safety of her hiding place. It was plain that Chanya was brainwashed. Instead of asking to see her right away, he had immediately betrayed her to Brother Lek and offered her up to the howling pack like a sacrificial lamb. How did Brother Lek exert such a hold over all these people—even her beloved Chanya? Cornelia wished she could dismiss Brother Lek as a nutcase. But his power over Chanya appalled her. She considered her options. If she ran, she would instantly attract the attention of the crowd. If she remained hidden, she risked eventually being found out. She was fast, but—

Someone seized her roughly by the arm and dragged her forward.

"Here she is!" Sister Lorraine shouted triumphantly, holding up Cornelia's arm like a prizefighter. "The Second Witness!" And with that, Lorraine promptly fainted.

A mob surrounded Cornelia and she found herself borne up on their shoulders and passed overhead as if she were in a mosh pit, until she had reached the marble portico where Brother Lek and Chanya were illuminated. As soon as her feet touched the porch,

Chanya pulled Cornelia into his spotlight and stepped outside it, leaving her alone and exposed.

"This *is* the face I saw in my dreams!" Chanya cried. "*This* is the Second Witness!" Cornelia tried desperately to make eye contact with Chanya, but he ignored her, his face glowing with perspiration. His eyes, Cornelia saw, were red-rimmed and glassy. He looked exhausted, and Cornelia's stomach clenched in fear.

"The Inner Sanctum is reserved for only the Two Most Worthy!" Chanya shouted.

"This is the Second Witness!" the crowd chanted. "The Second Witness is here!"

"Only the Second Witness can enter into Brother Lek's sanctuary!" Chanya roared. "Let. Her. Enter!"

"Let her enter!" the crowd screamed in frenzy.

Brother Lek clapped his hands sharply and stared at the throng, his expression unreadable behind the black glasses. As silence fell on the crowd, his glance flickered toward Cornelia and lingered on Chanya. Was he re-evaluating this new novice, Brother John, who had coincidentally appeared just before the "Second Witness" showed up? Or was he, too, like his followers, a true believer in this miraculous new development? The atmosphere remained thick with tension. Someone coughed, and the disciples stirred restlessly, like dogs on a leash. If Brother Lek said the wrong word, Cornelia thought the crowd might swarm the temple in unbridled hysteria.

"You are right," Brother Lek said calmly. "It *is* time."

The crowd seemed to sigh in unison, both in relief and expectation. As Brother Lek swung open the door to the temple, Cornelia was shocked to hear Chanya hissing in her ear.

"I believe he keeps *Satanic Christmas* in there. You must push it out a window and *go*." With that, he shoved Cornelia forward and she stumbled into the sanctuary. Behind her, Brother Lek shut the door, leaving her alone inside.

The windows were shuttered and the interior dark. The small room was hot and the air stale. A single light shone at the far end of the room, beneath which stood an easel and some jars of paint. Cornelia could see that the painting which stood on the easel was *Satanic Christmas.*

"It is time for the Second Witness to enter the sanctuary," Brother Lek repeated outside, his voice faint. "And to pass the test."

Pass the test? If Brother Lek was expecting Cornelia to have a vision and produce a sculpture like the other "novices," he was going to be sorely disappointed. The rest of the "temple" was unremarkable. A cot with rumpled sheets, a rectangular bamboo mat on the floor, a ceiling fan rotating above. A wooden chair and small metal desk with a few papers and books scattered haphazardly across it. A small dresser with several drawers left carelessly ajar. On top of the dresser stood a small framed photograph of three people, two men standing on either side of a woman. One of the men was Thai, but the other one, with his pale face and long brown hair parted in the middle, had the shaggy appearance of a 1960s hippie—

Brother Lek's muffled voice droned on outside.

"This is a special moment," he said. "For you. For me. For all of us. We all know what comes now."

One jarring note in the charmless decor was a television, VCR, and a stack of VHS tapes. Brother Lek was definitely behind the times.

Cornelia had an idea. She lifted *Satanic Christmas* down from the easel and laid it on the bamboo mat. The mat was the perfect size to wrap the painting in. At least it wouldn't attract so much attention, once she got away from here. It would be plain she was carrying something, but not what. Just another *farang* out shopping for treasures. But first she had to get out of here. Were the guards still on all sides of the building, or had they been drawn to the spectacle out front like everyone else? Cornelia would try the rear window first. That might be her best chance at absconding with the painting. And what about Chanya? Standing in the middle of this dark, dank room, with the painting lying at her feet, Cornelia felt something like euphoria. It wasn't because she'd found *Satanic Christmas,* or even Brother Lek. It was because Chanya had been faking it. He must have joined the cult to investigate. When he learned Cornelia was actually on the grounds, he had orchestrated this chance to get inside the sanctuary. But now that Cornelia had found *Satanic Christmas,* how would they escape? How much time did she have? Cornelia peered through the wooden shutters at Brother Lek in the spotlight. She felt a wave of sadness as she looked at him—slight, stiff, clad in black. From this angle, he looked underwhelming and un-Witness-like. *Was* he her grandfather? If he was, he was delusional. Chanya wasn't under the spell of Brother Lek, after all, which meant Brother Lek was a fake— didn't it? What about Miss Grace's haunting words from twenty years ago: "*Well, don't you think she, of all people, needs to know who the Two Witnesses are?*"

Was Miss Grace referring to the fact that the Two Paintings with their burdensome mystery would eventually belong to Cornelia? Or was Miss Grace hinting that Cornelia was more closely connected to the Two Witnesses than she could possibly imagine?

How could Cornelia leave without knowing whether or not Brother Lek was her long-lost grandfather? She shifted her stance as she peered out the shutters, trying to get a better look at Brother Lek's face. Was there a family resemblance?

"You all know when this photograph was taken," Brother Lek said, pointing toward the oversized poster of Brother Lek's sleeping face on the side of the temple.

"After your death!" someone called.

After his *death*? For the first time that night, Brother Lek smiled. Cornelia froze. Even with his sunglasses on, she recognized the smile: *Yim mee lessanai.* A smile which masks evil intent. The smile of malice which Sister Pen had warned Cornelia about: *If you see it, you must go.*

"And so it shall be for the Second Witness. First, she must enter the sanctuary. There she must sleep the sleep of the dead. If she awakens from it, and comes back out to us—"

Were they going to *kill* her? Cornelia watched Chanya spin away from Brother Lek and stare hard at the shuttered windows of the sanctuary, his expression panicked.

"But who will do the sacred duty of administering sleep to the Second Witness?"

"I will," Chanya said immediately, his voice tense. "It was my dream. It is my sculpture. Let me have the sacred duty of administering sleep to the Second Witness."

"Very well," Brother Lek agreed. "Brother John will enter. And administer the poison." He waved a small green glass bottle in the air. "The same poison that was administered to me. And it killed me." Brother Lek smiled again. "But not for long."

Hands trembling, Cornelia bundled up *Satanic Christmas* in the bamboo mat and moved toward the rear window. Her heart sank. Just outside, through a crack in the shutters, she saw a gun-toting guard. The guard still had his gun strapped across his chest, but now he was holding the torch in his hand as well. Chanya burst into the room. They both heard a distinctive click, and their eyes met.

"He has locked us in," Chanya said.

"So he expects you to—poison me?" Cornelia asked weakly.

"He offered me this," Chanya said. The small green bottle was in his hand, stoppered with a cork. "Do you smell—"

"Smoke," Cornelia said. Through the crack in the shutter, she saw the rear guard touching the corner of the temple with the torch. "The guards. They're using the torches. On all four corners."

"Brother John has sacrificed himself," Brother Lek shouted outside. "When the Second Witness emerges—"

"How can she survive both poison and fire?" someone wailed.

"If she is divine—" promised Brother Lek.

Cornelia looked around desperately—and saw it. Beneath the missing bamboo mat, where the bare floor now lay exposed, were hinges. It was a door, it seemed, into a crawl space beneath the house. Was it a death trap—or a way out? Cornelia lifted the door and practically jumped into the crawl space. She had been hoarding her phone battery, but it was time to use it. From the cell phone light, Cornelia was stunned to see that before her stretched a tunnel.

"It's a way out!" she called to Chanya, who was already lowering himself into the tunnel.

"I am right behind you," Chanya gasped.

Cornelia hesitated. "The painting—"

"Run," commanded Chanya. "The tunnel is filling with smoke. You must run!"

CHAPTER 19

THE DRAGON FESTIVAL

The tunnel seemed endless and the smoke was starting to overtake them.

"Faster!" Chanya urged.

Cornelia was running as fast as she could. She could hear Chanya coughing behind her. If only—

"Fresh air!" Chanya wheezed. "We must be close."

Cornelia emerged from the tunnel and looked around, blinking. Behind her, Chanya stepped out of the mouth of the giant snake sculpture in which Cornelia had hidden earlier. He turned and gazed at the predatory snake's gaping jaws and the helpless bird that was about to be devoured. "Brother Lek's escape hatch," he said. "In case he ever had to flee from his mad disciples."

Smoke billowed from the snake's mouth.

"We got out just in time," Cornelia said. "A few steps slower, and—"

"We must leave," Chanya said urgently. "When Brother Lek realizes our bodies are not in the ashes, he will know how we escaped, even if no one else does. He will come looking for us."

In the distance, Cornelia heard the strains of traditional music and drumming.

"The Dragon Festival," she said. "Lily mentioned it earlier. It's taking place right now on the Mekong River."

"You survived!"

Cornelia and Chanya whirled around to face Sister Lorraine, apparently recovered from her fainting spell, her face once again white as chalk.

"You *are* the Second Witness," Sister Lorraine breathed. "You just—*materialized* from the smoke." Sister Lorraine gaped in wonderment at Cornelia. "You're glowing," Sister Lorraine whispered.

"Sweating is more like it," Cornelia muttered.

"The Second Witness has appeared here to mark the spot where the great monument must be built," Chanya pronounced, drowning out Cornelia's comment.

Sister Lorraine turned wild-eyed toward Chanya. "Of *course*," she sighed. "This *is* the perfect spot. Right *here*." Then Sister Lorraine did a double-take. "And even *you* are alive, Brother John. How—"

"She raised me, of course," Chanya declared. "From the *dead*. She saved me. She is not of this earth. And you should be face-down before her. Do not speak. Do not look. Do not listen. *Pray*."

Sister Lorraine immediately fell face down on the ground and prostrated herself at Cornelia's feet. Chanya seized Cornelia's hand and they began, once again, to run.

The Dragon Festival Parade was already underway on the boulevard which ran alongside the Mekong River. Onlookers filled both sides of the boulevard and Chanya pulled Cornelia into their midst.

"Perhaps we might lose ourselves in the crowd," Chanya said. "At least long enough to catch a tuk-tuk to the border."

An all-girl band filled the street from curb to curb, beating rhythmically on long wooden drums made from water buffalo skins. The hour-glass-shaped drums were slung over the girls' shoulders, who were dressed identically in pink and white.

Chanya slapped a hand to his forehead. "My passport and everything are at the Mekong Guest House. We will have to stop there first."

The drumming girls filled the night air with an urgent cadence, as if the crowd were waiting expectantly for something. And they were. The Dragon Parade was no remembrance of things past. Instead, people from Laos and Thailand turned out in droves on both sides of the river to watch and wait for a great dragon to rise from the Mekong River's depths and make its appearance. It was a fire-breathing dragon, and fireballs erupted from the Mekong River and arced high into the air.

"Chanya," Cornelia pleaded. "*Wait.*" She clasped both his hands in her own and forced him to face her. Bewilderment flickered briefly in Chanya's anxious face.

"We cannot wait, Cornelia," Chanya said. "Brother Lek is dangerous. You could be in danger."

Cornelia wanted to throw her arms around Chanya right then and there. But there wasn't time. A young man in an ancient angel costume glided barefoot, hands folded, behind the girl drummers. He wore a gold head-piece in the shape of a dragon, and his bare torso sported golden wings, while blue silk trousers billowed from his waist to his knees.

"Chanya, the river will be packed with boats, won't it? Waiting for the fireballs?"

"Yes, of course, Cornelia," Chanya said, sounding impatient. "But we have no time to be tourists."

Now a band of young men playing traditional instruments passed by, plucking at pear-shaped, three-stringed lutes, clapping small cymbals together, and blowing on bamboo flutes.

"Chanya, I can't cross the border legally," Cornelia whispered as the band passed by, its tune lively and mournful at the same time. "I have no visa stamp. Pin-Pon brought me over."

Chanya seized Cornelia by her shoulders. She could see him mouth the word, *"Why?"* His voice was drowned out by the cheering crowds because the pinnacle of the parade had arrived. A large float featured a majestic green and gold dragon which appeared to be rippling through frothy waves.

"How could you do that?" Chanya shouted over the crowd. "This is *Laos*. Do you know what the prisons are like here?"

All around her, Cornelia heard a distinct murmuring. Many of the onlookers began to turn away from the dragon, pointing. In the night sky, billowing clouds glowed a fiery orange.

"Fire!" someone cried.

"Something's on fire!"

"The Ghost Garden! The Ghost Garden is burning!"

At that moment a group solemnly processed past, dressed completely in white, praying and bearing golden urns filled with yellow flowers. Chanya stepped smoothly into place behind the last row of white-robed marchers, pulling Cornelia with him. Clothed in white themselves and pressing their palms together in prayer, they blended in perfectly.

"Why did you sneak into Laos?" Chanya hissed angrily out of the side of his mouth as they marched.

"The Thai police were looking for me," Cornelia replied, keeping her eyes straight ahead.

"Why were the Thai police after you?" Chanya demanded.

"Somebody murdered Victor on the night train," Cornelia replied. "And stole *Apocalypse* from him. Which, of course, he had stolen from *me* in Missouri."

"And they believe it was *you?*" Chanya sounded horrified. There was a moment of stunned silence between them even as the frenzy of the crowd and the parade seemed to increase in intensity.

"I can't believe we left *Satanic Christmas* behind," Cornelia said bleakly. "After all we've gone through. And now it's burned. I can't seem to keep my hands on those paintings. It's like I'm cursed or something. Or the paintings are."

"The smoke almost devoured us," Chanya said severely. "If we'd been a few steps slower, we'd be lying dead in the tunnel right now. We had no choice but to leave it. You are more important than any painting."

Despite their dire circumstances, Chanya's words warmed Cornelia's heart.

"Look, we're almost to the Guest House," Cornelia muttered, stepping away from the parade and pulling Chanya with her onto the crowded sidewalk.

A moment later they had left the frenetic atmosphere of the boulevard behind and stood in the quiet side street leading to Ralph's bookstore and the Mekong Guest House. The street was dark, Ralph's bookstore closed.

"He's probably at the parade," Cornelia mumbled.

"Who?" Chanya asked. He looked nervously back toward the parade. "I guess no one is following us."

"Thank goodness for the Dragon Parade," Cornelia said. "It'd be hard to follow anyone in that mob scene."

"I am going to my room to get my passport," Chanya said. "Then we must go down to the river and see if we can hire someone to take us back across."

Cheerful white lights had been strung in the banana and coconut trees, but no one was sitting at the scattered wooden tables or in the hammocks. The courtyard had a desolate, abandoned air. The guests, along with Ian and Lily, must have been at the parade as well. Cornelia sank into a seat at one of the tables where a lonely white candle flickered inside a glass jar. For some reason, Cornelia couldn't get Father Bill out of her mind. It didn't matter that they had just narrowly escaped with their lives from Brother Lek. An image rose, unbidden, of those strange photographs of children lining the walls of the rectory, alongside the ancient icons of Jesus and the Virgin Mary. There was something about the juxtaposition that struck Cornelia as odd.

Miss Grace wrote in her letter that the first painting, *Satanic Christmas,* provided the identity of the Two Witnesses, while the second painting, *Apocalypse,* contained Their Warning to the World. And the identity of the Two Witnesses, which had upset Cornelia's grandmother and bewildered Miss Grace, was *O Seth to Lad of Krimiov.* Ralph had given Cornelia some food for thought about Seth—but what about Father Bill? He was a Catholic priest, after all, obsessed with acquiring certain pieces of religious art. Traveling the world in search of them. What might he know about the Two Witnesses, their Warning to the World, and *O Seth to Lad of Krimiov?* What had Sister Pen said about Father Bill, when Cornelia had asked her who the Two Witnesses were? *"It was Father Bill who led me to understand. He was the one who showed me—"*

Cornelia realized it was imperative that she complete her interrupted conversation with Father Bill.

Chanya emerged from his room to find Cornelia tucking her hair carefully back into her white nun's veil.

"Good idea," Chanya said approvingly. "The Thai police will not be looking for a nun."

"What about the Laotian police?" Cornelia asked. "Do you think they're looking for us?"

Chanya grimaced. "Brother Lek might have told the police we set the place on fire and fled," he admitted. "It wouldn't surprise me. He must explain himself somehow."

"All the more reason for us to get out of here," Cornelia said, heading for the crumbling stone steps leading down to the river. It was too much to hope that Pin-Pon might be loitering down there in his boat waiting for the festivities to begin. But surely someone would be willing to ferry them across the Mekong for the right price.

The crowd had spilled from the parade route down onto the river bank in anticipation of the appearance of the dragon fire in the Mekong River. Picnicking families had spread out bamboo mats while they waited. Vendors beneath umbrellas hawked sausages and fish balls on sticks along with roasted banana leaves stuffed with sticky rice. One vendor weaved expertly through the crowd carrying coiled dragon puppets whose red eyes flashed menacingly in the dark.

Cornelia felt a rush of relief when Pin-Pon's handsome profile came into view. Still as a statue in the moonlight, he posed serenely beside his wooden long tail boat looking out at the Mekong River. His grave expression brightened at the sight of Cornelia and Chanya approaching, but then his brow knitted in puzzlement.

"You became a nun?" he asked hesitantly. "In Laos?"

"Just part of the day's festivities," Chanya said cheerfully, jumping into Pin-Pon's boat. "The sisters invited Cornelia to...dance with them." Chanya held out his hand to help Cornelia into the boat as well.

Pin-Pon's frown deepened briefly before his face resumed its ordinary composed expression. If Chanya's explanation sounded dubious, Pin-Pon didn't let it show.

"Ready when you are, Pin-Pon," Chanya said heartily. Pin-Pon was still standing outside the boat.

"Don't you want to wait until after the dragon appears?" Pin-Pon asked calmly.

"Oh, but we want a better view from the middle of the river," Chanya explained. He added in a conciliatory tone, "If you don't mind."

Pin-Pon shrugged, seemingly indifferent. "It's very chaotic out there," he observed placidly, even as he shoved off from the shore.

Once they were on the river, and the shores of Laos receded behind them, Cornelia felt herself relax a little. Neither the Laotian police nor Brother Lek's minions appeared to be following. The river was filled with a procession of stately wooden boats, their masts and sails magnificently afire with flickering candles and lanterns, colorful flowers and wafting incense sticks, in honor of the rising dragon. Smaller boats floated on the margins, jockeying for a view of the dragon fire and the impressive parade of illuminated Oriental sailing ships. Pin-Pon's unassuming little boat was a barely noticed sliver slicing through the darkness. Cornelia was still careful to keep her head bowed modestly, like a nun, in case the occasional light from a passing boat fell on her.

Pin-Pon stood and poled his way gracefully through the swirling river traffic, while Chanya sat stiffly next to Cornelia. In the darkness, Cornelia could sense rather than see the strained expression on his face. Cornelia felt guilty, dragging Chanya into this mess. After all, he lived here. This was his home. If Cornelia was lucky, she might be able to slip out of the country and away from any trouble that was brewing. But if Chanya got into serious trouble with the law because of Cornelia...

Cornelia silently berated herself. I should have kept walking. I wish I'd never seen *Satanic Christmas*. I wish I could turn the clock back. I'd walk on the other side of the street, for starters. I'd never go near that trinket shop. It's a tourist trap. It really has turned out to be a trap for me, yanking me back to my past, maybe destroying my future. The police on both sides of the Mekong are probably after me. I don't even know if Brother Lek is really my grandfather. If he is my grandfather, he's completely mad. He's also a fraud. That secret tunnel helps explain how he died and rose from the dead. Just like I did. Like grandfather, like granddaughter.

Then, several things happened almost simultaneously. A deep roar erupted from the crowds on both sides of the river. Pin-Pon planted his pole and drew the boat to a sudden stop. He lifted a hand and pointed into the sky.

A ball of pink fire had arced upward out of the water and vanished into the air. Fire from the dragon's mouth. Fire from its nostrils. The dragon had surfaced and was spitting fire. The legend was that the dragon rose to celebrate the Buddha's return. The fireballs sailed through the sky over the Mekong , and if it wasn't really a fire-breathing dragon, no one had ever proven otherwise. Some scientists claimed methane gas was the culprit, others blamed tracer fire from Laotian soldiers. Whatever the truth was, more fireballs erupted from the river in rapid succession.

Cornelia lifted her head and followed a fireball's trajectory out of the dark waters of the Mekong and into the sky. How, really, to explain it? Like so much else that Cornelia had witnessed recently, the dragon fire was a complete mystery. This part of the world was deeply enigmatic to Cornelia, but the world she had come from, her own world, had become just as opaque. That was when she saw a police boat, blue lights flashing, speeding straight toward her.

Belatedly, it occurred to Cornelia that she had not only dragged Chanya into her mess, but also Pin-Pon. Loyal and trusting, he had no idea he was ferrying a wanted criminal and would no doubt be in serious trouble himself.

But the police boat bounced past them in the direction of an ascending fireball.

"Where are the police going?" Cornelia asked, her heart pounding.

"They are making sure no one is sending up the fire themselves," Pin-Pon explained. "They are patrolling for fakes. To guarantee the festival's authenticity."

"Well, let us get out of their way," Chanya said briskly. "I can see now why you didn't wish to be on the river when the dragon rose. This was a bad idea. Just take us back to Thailand."

Pin-Pon nodded as his pole sliced expertly through the water, and they began gliding silently toward Thailand.

CHAPTER 20
RETURN TO THE RECTORY

The chaotic river traffic and crowded river bank on the Thai side provided cover for their arrival, just as it had masked their departure from the Lao side. As the crowds *oohed* and *aahed*, pointing toward the sky and photographing the dragon fire spectacle, no one paid any attention when a stocky Thai man and a petite nun whose fair hair was concealed by her veil stepped out of a boat at the dark river's edge and melted into the crowds.

Without saying a word, Cornelia made a beeline for the rectory, which was only a few blocks away from the river. The crowd was thick near the riverbank, but gradually thinned out as they got further away.

"We must return to Bangkok," Chanya said, breathing heavily as he hurried to keep up with Cornelia's light-footed pace. "If the police really think you are involved in Victor's murder and the theft of *Apocalypse*, we must get you legal counsel immediately. Or possibly a one-way ticket back to the U.S."

Cornelia didn't slacken her step, but did deign to answer.

"What if Father Bill can help me clear this mystery up *and* clear my name? I think he may hold some missing pieces to this puzzle. I'm certain he doesn't think I killed Vic. Plus, he'll know if the Thai police are still looking for me. Besides, he just lives a few blocks away. Once we talk to him, we can go back to Bangkok. I promise."

"Unless I have a heart attack first," Chanya retorted.

"It's O.K.," Cornelia said, barely winded. "We're almost there."

The church and rectory sat on a quiet block. A lone dog barked in the distance. The rectory, like all the other houses on the block, was a traditional Thai house elevated on stilts. Water buffalo might have been stabled beneath the house in the past, but under Father Bill's house hung a couple of hammocks, a low wooden platform for sitting or lying, a rusted wheelbarrow, and a black bicycle leaning against a post. Just to the side of the house stood a large clay water pot, along with Father Bill's small Toyota pick-up. Although the church was dark, a light shone inside the rectory.

"Looks like maybe he's home and didn't go to the festival," Cornelia noted hopefully. She bounded up the wood stairs prepared to knock, but the door was already ajar.

"Father Bill," Cornelia called into the house. "Are you home? It's me, Cornelia." She pushed the door open wider and took a tentative step inside. "Sorry I left so abruptly, but I had to be somewhere important." Not a lie, Cornelia decided. "I wanted to finish our conversation, though." Make it sound casual, as if she had no idea she might be wanted for murder.

Chanya stepped around Cornelia and into the living room, which was crowded with its strange and exotic artwork. In the corner of the room, a lamp was lit next to a chair in which Father Bill was slumped and sleeping.

"He's asleep," Cornelia whispered.

Father Bill stirred slightly and moaned. His eyes fluttered open and locked on Cornelia.

"Sick," he whispered.

Cornelia rushed over and knelt down next to his chair. Father Bill's breathing was shallow and rapid.

"Father Bill, what's wrong? Is it a heart attack?"

"I don't know." Father Bill shook his head. "Something...I ate."

Cornelia glanced up at Chanya, who was staring at Father Bill's pale, perspiring face.

"Drive me to the hospital," Father Bill wheezed.

"We don't have a car," Cornelia said desperately.

"I do."

They helped the stricken priest stagger to his pick-up and slide inside, where he slumped between Chanya and Cornelia. Father Bill was sweating profusely and clutching his stomach. Chanya shoved the truck into gear and they lurched away.

"You're...a nun," Father Bill whispered.

Cornelia pulled the veil from her hair. "Father Bill, what did you eat? They'll need to know at the hospital."

"I don't know," Father Bill panted. "Just tea."

"Are you sure? What about dinner?"

Father Bill weakly shook his head. "We just had tea," he said cryptically.

"Who did you have tea with?" Cornelia asked. "Maybe he'll remember what you ate."

Father Bill groaned. "Why did you leave? I had to tell you. Ask you."

"I was afraid the police might suspect me," Cornelia confessed. "It was stupid of me to run like that. What did you want to tell me? Tell me now. I'm listening." Cornelia squeezed his hand. She hoped she was giving him an encouraging *yim suu suu* smile.

"Look at that," Father Bill moaned.

Cornelia looked around, bewildered.

"Chanya, I think he's hallucinating," Cornelia said despairingly. When she looked back, Father Bill was staring directly at Cornelia. Then he turned his gaze on Chanya.

"The Two Witnesses," Father Bill mumbled.

"We're here," Chanya announced, as the truck screeched to a stop in front of the hospital entrance.

"Do you know who the Two Witnesses are?" Cornelia asked lightly. "All I know is the clue my grandmother left me. *O Seth to Lad of Krimiov.*" Cornelia knew she was chattering from nervousness, but maybe she could snap Father Bill out of his feverish state. "Have you heard of that? Do you know what it is? It sounds Russian, doesn't it?" Father Bill was watching Cornelia again, his eyes peculiarly bright.

"Maybe it's a Russian book title?" Cornelia speculated. "A folk song? A painting?"

"A Russian painting," Father Bill breathed. "Yes. I see now. What she did."

Chanya had thrown his car door open and leapt out, calling for help. Several orderlies were rushing their way.

"It's a Russian painting?" Cornelia repeated, surprised. But Father Bill was confused. He was ill.

"It's an...an...a.." Father Bill's voice trailed off as hospital staff pulled him from the car and onto a stretcher.

"Cornelia," Father Bill called weakly as they rolled him into the hospital. He offered up a brief, brilliant smile. "It's in my house."

Cornelia stood in the middle of Father Bill's living room and looked around. Chanya had driven her back to the rectory after the doctor and nurses had pumped Father Bill's stomach and sedated him. He was in serious condition, but the doctor thought his chances for recovery were fair. A police detective had interviewed them before they left the hospital.

"The doctor says he appears to have eaten too many Thai dragon peppers," the detective said. "Celebrating the Dragon Fire Festival. But neither of you partook?" He looked quizzically at Chanya and Cornelia.

"No, neither of us partook," Chanya confirmed.

The policeman shook his head and clucked his tongue. "*Farangs* are foolish to think they can handle such extreme spice. Especially a *farang* who has lived in Thailand too long. They become over-confident. Even Thais can be overcome by too many dragon peppers. He has all the symptoms. Hallucinations, vomiting, loss of consciousness. He's lucky you brought him here in time. Lucky you were celebrating with him all evening, but didn't help him eat the dragon peppers."

Chanya and Cornelia exchanged glances. With him all evening?

"We were looking for a foreign woman who was seen on the night train. She wore a headscarf and sunglasses which concealed her hair and face. She wore long sleeves and a long skirt. A witness claimed to see her carry a bulky package off the train and get into a black car. But now we know it was just you. Father Bill said you got into his car with your suitcase. And then Chanya joined both of you and you spent the evening enjoying the festival. That's all the Father could tell us before he lost consciousness." The detective sighed. "A *farang* collapsed and died on the night train. A witness thought they spotted a foreign woman near him, or with him, maybe even having a drink with him, so we wanted to question her." The detective scrutinized Cornelia. "*Did* you see anything or talk to anyone? Other than Father Bill?"

Cornelia blinked. The detective was looking at her oddly. She wondered if she was smiling, and if her smile was revealing. "No, I didn't see anything. And I didn't talk to anyone," she added truthfully. "Other than Father Bill."

The detective frowned. "We must put a lid on the wild rumors. Rumors of murder and robbery of a foreign tourist on the night train! Nonsense! The *farang* was old and overweight. He smoked and drank too much. His own Thai in-laws admitted as much. They claimed he was carrying something valuable with him on the train that went missing. Some priceless treasure he'd brought back with him from America," the detective said sarcastically. "Wishful thinking on their part. Just another gambling fool chasing a pot at the end of the rainbow. Full of grand schemes and illusions." He narrowed his eyes at Cornelia accusingly. "And so because you were on the train, you became the *farang's* murderess. And thief." The detective snorted derisively. Cornelia forced a smile. She, for whom smiles normally came so easily.

"I hope your priest survives his run-in with the dragon peppers," the detective said disapprovingly. "By the way, did you see the fire?"

"What fire?" Cornelia asked, feigning ignorance.

"Oh, the fire!" Chanya exclaimed brightly. "Yes, of course, across the river. We saw smoke. What happened?"

"You didn't hear?" the detective said. "The Garden of Ghosts burned to the ground and Brother Lek has vanished."

"Vanished?" Cornelia swallowed.

The detective nodded importantly, clearly relishing delivering such dramatic news. "Yes. Vanished into thin air. Or perhaps his body is in the rubble." The detective winced. "They are still sifting through the ashes. The rest of his people appear to have gotten out. They are all leaving. The government is shutting it all down. The cult is being dissolved as we speak." The detective chuckled. "There are crazy rumors swirling around about Two Witnesses. Crazy religious nonsense. Brother Lek claimed to be one Witness, and some of the survivors claim another Witness appeared there tonight as well. The one they were all waiting for. The *second* Witness. But no sign of *that* witness either," the detective remarked wryly. "Naturally."

Back in Father Bill's house, the room was hot and stuffy despite wooden shutters thrown open to the night. A brown ceramic teapot and two white cups were upside down on the draining board, recently washed and rinsed. The air outside was completely still. Sweat trickled down Cornelia's back. A dookay lizard's mournful cry wafted through the open window, while the pungent smoke from a burning mosquito coil lingered inside the house. "Father Bill really covered for me," Cornelia said. "Telling the police I was on the train with him the whole time, that we were with him here all night. He gave me an alibi for Vic's murder, and he gave us both an alibi for the fire at the Stone Garden." The room felt empty of the priest's imposing presence but crowded with his haunting pictures. The pictures of the ghostly children and their strange expressions. What were they staring at? What did they see?

"Perhaps," Chanya said slowly. "Or maybe he was just confused in his delirium. After all, you *did* get into his car and go back to the rectory with him to talk about Vic and the painting. Maybe he really did think you spent the evening celebrating with him. What did he say about having tea with someone?"

"You're right. He and I did have coffee. Maybe he was thinking of *me* in his feverish state when he mentioned having tea with someone." Cornelia frowned. "But a witness really did see a woman get off the train wearing a headscarf and carrying a bulky package and get into a black car. *I* wasn't wearing a headscarf. My little backpack wasn't particularly bulky. And Father Bill has an old, beat-up blue Toyota pick-up. *Was* there another foreign woman on the train that night who poisoned Vic and stole the painting?"

"Eyewitnesses are notoriously terrible with details. Perhaps somewhere, deep in his sub-conscious, the eyewitness believed a black car was appropriate for a murderous foreign woman. So the eyewitness embellished, unintentionally, about the black car and bulky package. Maybe it was just you getting into Father Bill's pick-up."

A gust of wind blew into the room, rustling papers on Father Bill's desk and rattling his perpetual Scrabble game. Outside, palm tree fronds blew wildly in the sudden wind, as if they were agitated. The wind had knocked the letter **V** askew on the Scrabble board, and Cornelia straightened it. Four points. She spotted another high-value letter, **K,** and touched it. She began re-arranging letters until she had spelled out, *O Seth to Lad of Krimiov.*

Right before Father Bill was rolled into the hospital, he had told Cornelia that *something* was in his house. They had been talking about *O Seth to Lad of Krimiov.* Cornelia's grandmother claimed the words revealed the identity of the Two Witnesses. Father Bill had said it was a Russian painting. Did the painting even exist? Or had Father Bill been hallucinating?

Cornelia had a disturbing thought. "For all we know, maybe Father Bill killed Vic. Father Bill *was* on the train, after all. He told me he had been in a meeting in Bangkok. I didn't even ask him, he just volunteered the information. Maybe he killed Vic because Vic stole *Satanic Christmas* from him, *and* because Father Bill wanted *Apocalypse.*" Something else occurred to Cornelia. "He said the strangest thing to me when I was talking to him earlier. He said, "*Who stole* Satanic Christmas *from your friend who was keeping it safe for you? Why would Vic steal the same painting twice?*"

"It didn't make any sense for *Vic* to steal the painting from Father Bill, sell it, and then steal it *again* from you, Chanya. Especially since Vic was still trying to get from Missouri to Bangkok. But it makes sense if Father Bill stole *Satanic Christmas* from you. He was trying to get *Satanic Christmas* back after Vic had stolen it from him." Cornelia felt uneasy. "If that's the case, Father Bill was trying to throw me off his scent with his question: *Who stole* Satanic Christmas *from your friend?* He was pretending to help me discover the thief's identity, so he'd be the last person I'd suspect. It worked, too." Cornelia looked slowly around the room at the picture-covered walls. "It fits his M.O. Father Bill clearly covets strange religious art. Including my grandmother's paintings. And he can't have that much money to be throwing around on precious artwork."

"It's perfectly possible. But how did *Satanic Christmas* get from Father Bill to Brother Lek?" Chanya mused. "Father Bill does not seem like the type to sell the art for profit. He seems to want to surround himself with it." Chanya studied the wall of photographs. The largest was clearly a copy of a very old photograph. Two girls and a boy stood side by side, frowning at the camera. The girls wore long skirts and long shawls over their hair, the boy a rather elaborate and old-fashioned cap which flopped jauntily to one side.

"I wonder when and where this picture was taken," Cornelia said.

"Fatima, Portugal," Chanya pronounced.

"How do you know?"

"It says so right here," Chanya shrugged. "Below the picture."

"Are all the pictures labeled?" Cornelia felt a stirring of excitement.

The next photograph on the wall was a black-and-white photograph of four girls on their knees, faces upturned and glowing, as if they were awestruck at what they were seeing. There was no sign in the photograph, however, of precisely what it was that so mesmerized the girls.

"Garabandal, Spain," Chanya read.

The photograph after that was obviously much more recent, and in color. In this picture, four girls and two boys posed much like the four girls in the previous photo: on their knees, staring dumbstruck into the sky, at...nothing.

"Medjugorje, Yugoslavia," Chanya said.

In each of these pictures, onlookers crowded around the children. The onlookers were either openly scrutinizing the children, or looking with bewildered expressions in the same direction as the children. Obviously, the crowd did not see whatever it was the children themselves saw.

Similar photographs covered the entire wall; there were additional pictures of the children of Fatima, Garabandal, and Medjugorje. There were also pictures of other children. In every picture, although the children's knees were planted firmly on the ground, their upturned faces gave off an almost ghostly glow, as if they were peering into another dimension at something unimaginable.

"Why did he collect these weird pictures of these kids?" Cornelia wondered aloud. Outside, a tropical downpour had begun. The dookay lizard's mating call had been extinguished by the rain, and no doubt the high spirits of revelers had been dampened by the deluge as well. Cornelia shifted her gaze to the bookcase next to Father Bill's chair. She reached out and swept her fingers along the spines of books, soft and hardcover, old and new.

"Hey, listen to this title," Cornelia said. *From Fatima to Medjugorje: Visions of Jesus and Mary in the 20th Century.*

"Visions," Chanya said. "That explains the looks on the children's faces."

"Visions of Jesus and Mary," Cornelia noted. "In places called Fatima, and Garabandal, and Medjugorje. That explains why Father Bill was interested. A Catholic thing."

"Same here," Chanya said, gesturing at the adjoining wall. On this wall, however, there were no old photographs of spellbound, haunted children. Instead, a patchwork of differently-sized pictures crowded the wall, all of them apparently images of Jesus and Mary painted hundreds, if not thousands, of years before. In all of these ancient paintings, the Virgin Mary was holding an infant or child Jesus in her arms. *Our Lady of the Sign. Our Lady of the Monastery of the Caves. Our Lady of the Don. Our Lady of Kykkos.*

"Look," Cornelia said excitedly. "Father Bill mentioned a *Russian* painting. Look at this. *Our Lady of Vladimir "The Planting of the Tree of Russian Sovereignty."*

In the center of the painting was Mary holding the child Jesus. Something like a family tree sprouted outward from Jesus and Mary, the multitude of branches bearing images of Russian...saints? priests? holy men? At any rate, there were many bearded men, holding scrolls, some of them wearing hats and adorned with crosses.

"Father Bill's pictures may all be Russian," Chanya said thoughtfully. "Or many of them, anyway. Russian Orthodox icons. Religious pictures. Holy pictures."

"Vladimir is a Russian name, isn't it? A Russian city, maybe? Here's another Vladimir picture. *Theotokos of Vladimir,*" Cornelia pointed out. "But nothing which says *O Seth to Lad of Krimiov.*" She sank into Father Bill's empty chair. "I can't put it all together. It doesn't make any sense." The steady sound of falling rain filled the room, and the air had cooled noticeably.

"No," Chanya agreed tiredly. "It doesn't." He frowned. "I need to phone Bangkok and check my messages. I think the Enlightenment Trust has been trying to reach me, with details about their ceremony, honoring the slum project. But the cult confiscated my cell phone. I presume it's long gone now. Probably melted in the fire. Do you have yours?"

"Yes," Cornelia said. "We don't want to miss that ceremony. I told you I'd be back for it. You need to be back for it, too!" She pressed the power button. The screen on her phone flickered to life. Cornelia stared, uncomprehending, at the image that swam into view.

"Satanic Christmas," she said.

"I know," Chanya said somberly. "I'm sorry we lost it. I know your grandmother painted it and—"

"Satanic Christmas!" Cornelia shouted, jumping up from the chair. "I took a picture of *Satanic Christmas* with my phone. I have a copy of it. I'd forgotten, but here it is. My phone screen rotates through the pictures I've taken. Look, maybe it's not a great picture, but still. Miss Grace said *Satanic Christmas* revealed the identity of the Two Witnesses." She peered closely at the small image on her phone. "I wish we had a way to upload it to Father Bill's computer so we can enlarge it and look at it more closely. But I didn't bring a connector or charger or anything. I was in such a hurry to get up here."

"Send it to your e-mail, or to mine, and we can open it and look at it on Father Bill's computer," Chanya suggested.

Cornelia gleefully threw her arms around Chanya's neck. "Chanya, you're a genius!" she cried.

"Not really," Chanya said modestly. But he looked pleased at the compliment anyway. They stood face-to-face for a moment, neither of them moving, as the rain drummed loudly on the roof. Cornelia released Chanya from her embrace, stepped back, and turned toward Father Bill's computer. A few minutes later, they were both hunched at Father Bill's computer, looking at an enlarged image of *Satanic Christmas*.

They Will Gloat and Exchange Gifts With Glee Once the Two Witnesses Are Dead.

"This painting is...disturbing," Chanya remarked.

Cornelia laughed. "That's an understatement."

Chanya reached out and touched the computer screen, as if physical contact might communicate the image's secrets to them. "Was it burned in a fire or something? It looks discolored, warped. Is that a deliberate effect?"

"Deliberate, I'm sure," Cornelia said. "So much for a warm-and-fuzzy Christmas. Instead of cheerful red and green colors, there are these dark, sticky patches of red and black. Like pools of congealing blood and hot tar. But if you look closer, these are Christmas gifts that everyone is exchanging."

Chanya enlarged the image and zeroed in on the menacing-looking gifts being exchanged by the throngs depicted in the painting. The celebrating crowds at the top of the painting grinned as they gleefully traded obscene parodies of Christmas presents. One unnaturally tall man resembled a semi-naked Santa who at first offered what appeared to be a gift to a child. Upon closer inspection, though, it was apparent that "Santa" was hurling something like molten iron into the child's shocked and blistered face. And the people's celebratory expressions changed. Yes, even though it was a painting and not a video, nevertheless the painting was not *static*. The viewing experience was more akin to watching a film. As Chanya scrolled down, the gloating grins grew imperceptibly fainter. The further down the painting Chanya scrolled, the less jubilant the crowd appeared. Brazen confidence faded to uncertainty. The transformation seemed to pick up speed as the viewer's gaze descended. The faces in the crowd morphed into surprise, then shock, then horror. It was as if the viewer plummeted downward from a great height, watching as he fell while the crowd dissolved into frenzied terror—a mirror image of himself.

Chanya began to read: "Men out of every people, race, language and nation will stare at their corpses, for three-and-a-half days, not letting them be buried, and the people of the world will be glad about it and celebrate the event by giving presents to each other, because these two prophets have been a plague to the people of the world."

Cornelia shifted her gaze to the cramped, old-fashioned black script that clogged every available inch which was not already crammed with the disturbing images. Chanya zoomed in on the script so they both could read it.

"After the three-and-a-half days, God breathed life into them and they stood up, and everybody who saw it happen was terrified; then they heard a loud voice from heaven say to them, "Come up here", and while their enemies were watching, they went up to heaven in a cloud. Immediately, there was a violent earthquake, and a tenth of the city collapsed; seven thousand persons were killed in the earthquake, and the survivors, overcome with fear, could only praise the God of heaven."

"What is the rectangular border that runs around the entire painting?" Chanya asked. "It looks like your grandmother painted a frame around the painting. It's like a chain, or necklace." Chanya leaned closer, squinting. "Look at those tiny rectangles that make up the frame. They're all linked together like a necklace. Jewels? Beads?"

"I think it's a rosary," Cornelia said. "Father Bill mentioned it when I asked him about the crucifix. See?" She pointed to the small crucifix at the very bottom of the painting, in the center. "The crucifix hangs from the chain. So maybe those are rosary beads which encircle the painting. I didn't understand why Miss Grace would paint a crucifix, but it doesn't make any more sense for my grandmother to. Neither of them was Catholic. Try enlarging the beads."

Chanya tapped a key to increase the magnification, and the miniature rectangles which bordered the painting increased to the size of postage stamps.

Chanya let out a low whistle. It did indeed look like a rosary framed the painting, only the "beads" were a long chain of linked television screens. "Look at that. TV screens. Or computer screens."

"Yes," Cornelia marveled. "Inside every rosary bead there's a tiny person sitting in front of every single screen. You can see their silhouette in front of each screen."

"Men of every people, race, language and nation will stare at their corpses for three-and-a-half days," Chanya repeated thoughtfully. He gently tapped the screen. "Look. All the rectangles, the miniature computer screens, are identical. What's being broadcast? What's *inside* those tiny screens?"

"The whole world is staring at the corpses of the Two Witnesses," Cornelia replied. "Like a live feed from one of those disaster scenes."

"Or like propaganda from a totalitarian state," Chanya remarked.

"But then the scene changes," Cornelia continued, getting into the spirit of their narration. "Suddenly. Shockingly. Those dead bodies rise. The State has lost control. The world goes from euphoria to terror and awe." Cornelia snapped her fingers. "In one instant."

"Let's take a closer look at the TV screens running along the top of the painting," Chanya said. "Make them even bigger."

He zoomed in closer on the rosary beads, until the screens revealed two crumpled, blood-soaked bodies lying abandoned in a street. One of the corpses clearly wore trousers, while the other wore a long skirt. Everything in the picture—the man, the woman, the street and sky—were in black and white. But grisly red splotches on the clothes gave the appearance of dried blood.

"The bodies of a man and a woman," Cornelia declared. "Now round the corner and move down the right side of the border."

"Wow," Chanya remarked as he moved the cursor down the right side of the painting. "Your grandmother must have been so skilled to paint such tiny, detailed figures. Almost like photographs." He peered more closely. "Maybe she drew them with pen and ink."

"Yes. Portrait miniatures. In pen and ink." Cornelia snapped open the oval silver locket her grandmother had given her when she was a child. "This is a portrait miniature of my father. My grandmother gave it to me after he died. She always told me Miss Grace drew it for me." Cornelia sighed. "This is what my grandmother added to the painting. Miss Grace said in her letter that Grandma had added something before she died, had finally finished the painting, had finally identified the Two Witnesses. Grandma painted the rosary beads which run around the edges of the painting. Inside each rosary bead, she drew a tiny TV screen containing the Two Witnesses." Cornelia paused. "Miss Grace noticed the crucifix at the bottom of the painting, but not being Catholic, she didn't recognize that the border around the painting was made up of rosary beads. Father Bill recognized the rosary, but missed the miniature scene inside each rosary bead. Miss Grace said it almost killed Grandma to finish it. I guess it really did, since she died soon after."

The gawkers continued to stare at the unmoving corpses down the right side of the painting. But as Chanya moved the cursor around the lower right corner and along the bottom of the painting, the miniature image inside the screens changed. The man and woman, their backs to the camera, now hovered upright, floating above the dusty street. They were still in black-and-white, but the red stains had transformed to radiant white, as if bursts of light now emanated from the deadly wounds. The silhouettes of the viewers had changed, too. Now the viewers were shown in profile, heads thrown back, mouths agape, in shock and terror.

"After the three-and-a-half days, God breathed life into them and they stood up, and everybody who saw it happen was terrified," Chanya recited. He paused the cursor at the lower left corner of the painting and looked at Cornelia. Through the open window, the downpour had passed, and rain dripped from the trees. The night was alive with the manic energy of frogs and insects.

"Go ahead," Cornelia said. "Let's see who the Two Witnesses are."

CHAPTER 21
THE MURDERER

"You look perfect," Cornelia said, beaming.

The taxi pulled away from the curb, leaving Chanya and Cornelia standing together on a quiet, tree-lined Bangkok *soi*, in front of a stately colonial-era home surrounded by a high concrete wall. An elaborate wrought-iron gate featured Lakhon dancers crowned with Chada headdresses, their delicate fingers curved unnaturally backward.

Chanya looked uncomfortable in a suit and tie and tugged nervously at his shirt collar. His short black hair, recently cut and just washed, was slicked down.

"Let's get inside to the air conditioning before we start to wilt," Cornelia urged. "We want you fresh for the reception."

After Chanya had been able to access his phone messages again, he'd learned the details of the reception of The Enlightenment Trust, honoring those who were doing extraordinary work among the poor and suffering. According to the embossed invitation, which had been mailed to Chanya's office, he would be honored along with two others—a Buddhist monk and a Catholic nun. In addition to the recognition, each honoree would receive a handsome cash award to spend on their good work. It was the extra money that Chanya was most thrilled about—money he could spend improving the dormitories and kitchen. Money to fund a small library, computer room, and study carrels so the children could have a quiet, designated place for study. Money to spend on scholarships to send some of the older children on to boarding schools or university.

Chanya was not as thrilled about being publicly honored. Cornelia knew he was most comfortable when he was up to his elbows in the sweaty turmoil and daily drama of the slum, putting his passion to work on behalf of the disenfranchised and vulnerable. A suit and tie felt like a strait jacket on him, and having to watch his words in the presence of the rich and powerful left him feeling similarly strait-jacketed. Cornelia was actually relieved to learn that Chanya did not have to give a speech. She feared that if he began to talk, his passion and temper might get the best of him, and he might end up alienating those who were giving him such a generous financial gift. The chairman of The Enlightenment Trust did ask that Chanya prepare a Power Point presentation of his work in the slum. This was the perfect solution since Chanya could project the needs and the successes of his project on the screen without saying a word.

The reception was being held at the home of a wealthy Thai businessman, Boon-Mee Pornpipatpong, who also served as a board member of The Enlightenment Trust. Cornelia was surprised when the door was opened by a tall, gray-haired American woman, who turned out to be the Thai businessman's wife. Though a *farang,* she was elegantly dressed in a shimmering green traditional Thai *Chakri* dress, which was interwoven delicately with gold silk.

"I am Nan Rotham Pornpipatpong," she said pleasantly. "Please call me Nan. We're delighted to be able to honor you here today." After Chanya introduced Cornelia, Nan glanced shrewdly at her. "Be careful. I also came to Thailand when I was young and idealistic. I made the mistake of falling in love with a handsome young

Thai man and I've never left." She smiled. "Now let me introduce you to the other honorees."

Cornelia found herself face to face with a short, wiry Buddhist monk of international renown named Ajahn Preecha, who wore round spectacles and lived in a cave on an island in the Andaman Sea, where suffering pilgrims visited to find solace and peace. He was said to be able to heal mental illness, drug addiction and depression with merely a glance, and Cornelia felt his piercing gaze on her during the introductions. Cornelia suspected that he, like Nan, was wondering where Cornelia fit into the picture. Chanya introduced her as his "co-worker."

"She has stayed longer and helped me more than anyone else, both with the planning and the day-to-day execution," Chanya explained stiffly, as if he had rehearsed. It occurred to Cornelia that Chanya was so nervous he no doubt *had* rehearsed his responses to possible questions.

Cornelia smiled somewhat uncomfortably at the monk, remembering not to shake his hand, but instead bowing her head with her hands folded, as a gesture of respect.

Their hostess Nan interrupted the awkward moment. "Ah, and here is our third honoree."

Cornelia turned and was shocked to see, for the first time since the fire, Sister Pen.

"Sister Penprapa worked for years in the slums of Bangkok, before being assigned to help the poor and suffering children of Laos," Nan explained. "Most recently, as she has grown older, Sister Penprapa has entered a cloister to devote herself to prayer." Nan added, "She received special permission to attend this ceremony honoring her for her life's work."

Chanya reached out and enfolded tiny Sister Pen in his thick arms, giving her a forceful bear hug. "We go way back," he muttered, his voice catching. Sister Pen looked both startled and pleased, her eyes blinking owlishly behind her thick glasses.

"Why, that's wonderful," Nan remarked. "I had no idea. Now, really, you all must take a seat and have a cup of jasmine tea or a glass of champagne before the ceremony starts. We have some delicious satay, spring rolls and fish balls which will be brought round momentarily. And you should try the trio of dipping sauces."

Sister Pen seized Cornelia's hand and pulled her down into the chair beside her. "My dear, I have wondered about you often, and how it went that night. I'm very grateful, of course, for the short e-mail you sent assuring me you were back in Thailand and safe after the fire. And I'm so pleased to see you and Chanya here, safe and well."

"I wanted to give you more details about our adventure," Cornelia said. "But I wasn't sure how closely the government monitored your communications, and I didn't want to put you at more risk. You'd already helped me so much in finding Chanya. I'm glad you're here."

"You're so thoughtful, dear," Sister Pen said warmly. She looked intently at Cornelia. "But now that we are face to face, you must tell me everything."

"Yes. But first, I have some questions of my own," Cornelia said. "I asked you that night who the Two Witnesses actually were. You had created them in your topiary, after all. You had created the True Witnesses from the Bible, rather than Brother Lek's false witnesses. You had created a man and a woman. And you told me Father Bill had shown you...something about the identity of the Two Witnesses. Then we were interrupted." Cornelia paused and pulled her phone out of her purse. She powered it on and began scrolling through her stored images. When she'd found what she was looking for, she held it up to Sister Pen. "Is this what he showed you?"

The image which Cornelia displayed to Sister Pen was the same image that Cornelia's grandmother had drawn repeatedly, in miniature, along the left edge of *Satanic Christmas*. It was the image she had painstakingly sketched inside each rosary bead, the image which filled the tiny TV screens. Astonishingly, it was also the same image hanging on the wall of Father Bill's sparse little living room.

Theotokos of Vladimir hung there that night, grave and ancient, above Father Bill's messy table, which was littered with a spoon and bowl, a few pieces of mail, a book, and the Scrabble board. It was the exact same portrait that Cornelia's grandmother had reproduced in miniature along the left edge of *Satanic Christmas*, over and over and over. "Men of every people, race, language and nation will stare at their corpses for three-and-a-half days," the Book of Revelation declared. In *Satanic Christmas*, individuals sat transfixed before their thumbnail-sized computer screens, staring at the bloodied corpses of the Two Witnesses—who are revealed upon resurrection as Jesus Christ and his mother Mary.

"It matches," Chanya had said wonderingly. "The image from *Satanic Christmas* of the Two Witnesses matches the *Theotokos of Vladimir* painting. It's the same painting."

Cornelia had glanced down at Father Bill's Scrabble board beneath the painting, where she'd earlier spelled out, *O Seth to Lad of Krimiov*. "So what does this mean? Grandmother said *O Seth to Lad of Krimiov* was the identification of the Two Witnesses. I thought maybe it was a Russian painting. But the painting my grandmother copied is *Theotokos of Vladimir*, not *O Seth to Lad of Krimiov*." Cornelia frowned and touched the letter K on the Scrabble board, then the letter V. She looked up at Chanya, excited. "Chanya. Look." After a few moments, she had re-arranged the letters in *O Seth to Lad of Krimiov* to spell *Theotokos of Vladimir*.

"It's an anagram," Cornelia said to Chanya. "My grandmother wrote the identity of the Two Witnesses as an anagram. She just re-arranged the letters of *Theotokos of Vladimir* to spell *O Seth to Lad of Krimiov*. That's what Father Bill was trying to tell me earlier tonight. He said, *"It's an...It's an..."* He realized it was an anagram. Her reproduction of the portrait was so small, and maybe she didn't trust herself to copy it accurately, or for others to ever identify it. So she left an extra clue."

What was it her grandmother had once said about Miss Grace? *Really, she's just a mystery lover at heart. She loves a good puzzle...I suppose we all get it from our Creator. Sometimes I think God loves strewing the clues. We end up tracking them.*

Grandmother herself had left an extra clue, in order to confirm to Cornelia that she was on the right track.

"I wonder why she felt the need to mask the answer with an anagram," Cornelia said. "Why not just write *Theotokos of Vladimir*? Maybe Grandmother wasn't one hundred percent sure she was right, and this was one more safeguard against passing on bad information? After all, she always said that she didn't fully understand all that she painted, and only God really knew."

"Maybe," Chanya agreed. "But I think she left the anagram just for you. To confirm to you that you had discovered the Two Witnesses. She knew you'd never decipher the anagram until you had already identified the image in the rosary as T*heotokos of Vladimir*. It was her way of letting you know that you were right, in case you doubted. She trusted *you* with the identity of the Two Witnesses, but she didn't trust art critics, and journalists, and dealers, and art thieves. She didn't trust all those with their own agendas. She didn't want to cast pearls before swine. So in case the answer fell into the wrong hands, she disguised it." Chanya smiled. "She knew you would deduce the answer eventually."

"Only thanks to your help," Cornelia pointed out. She and Chanya gazed silently at the painting before them, pondering what it meant.

Theotokos of Vladimir depicted the boy Jesus resting trustingly on the cheek of a solemn-eyed Virgin Mary. *Theotokos*—the Mother of God, the birth-giver of God. And the child-God himself, seeking solace in her embrace.

Now, at The Enlightenment Trust reception, Cornelia's phone shimmered with the primitive sorrow and tenderness of *Theotokos of Vladimir.* Sister Pen looked gravely at the image, and then at Cornelia.

"Yes," Sister Pen answered simply. "This is what Father Bill showed me."

"But I don't understand," Cornelia said. "What does it all mean? How does this painting reveal the identity of the Two Witnesses in the Book of Revelation?"

"You saw the photographs which covered the walls of Father Bill's house?" Sister Pen queried.

"The children around the world who have had visions of the Virgin Mary and Jesus," Cornelia affirmed.

"Father Bill has been researching these visions, and their accompanying messages, for decades," Sister Pen explained. "He has been trying to piece together the puzzle of it all. The *why* of it. Why would Jesus be appearing with his mother in all corners of the world throughout the twentieth century, and even now? What is the essence of their message?"

"And what *is* the essence of their message?" Cornelia asked cautiously.

"Well, there is much to be said about that, and Father Bill, rest his soul, could give you a fuller picture. But certainly, it is a warning."

Cornelia had a sudden recollection of Miss Grace's letter to her, recounting her grandmother's final words about the identity of the Two Witnesses which God had at last revealed to her. "Oh, Grace, we have been wrong. We have been blind." Because the Two Witnesses of the Book of Revelation were not Moses and Elijah? Were not Elijah and Enoch? Were not two old men in white beards at all? Because the Two Witnesses included not only Jesus, but his mother Mary? An uncontroversial proposition, perhaps, for a Roman Catholic priest like Father Bill, but for a Pentecostal lady preacher and an Ozark outsider artist, this was earthshaking news indeed.

"So Father Bill believes these repeated appearances of Jesus and his mother is what the Book of Revelation speaks about when it speaks about the Two Witnesses of the End Times?" Cornelia asked. "And Grandmother chose *Theotokos of Vladimir,* but she might have copied any painting of Jesus and his mother?"

Sister Pen nodded. "Yes."

Cornelia narrowed her eyes at Sister Pen. "Do you agree with his theory?"

Sister Pen smiled. "Oh, I think he's right about that. But there may be more to this than meets the eye. The identities of the Two Witnesses are a great mystery. You know the mysteries of God cannot be contained. And so often these mysteries repeat themselves, like ever-widening circles which ripple outward from the first splash. Biblical scholars have often identified the Two Witnesses as Moses and Elijah. The witness of the Law, represented by Moses, and the witness of the Prophets, represented by Elijah. Moses gives us God's Law, Elijah warns us of the consequences of ignoring it. These two men also appeared at Jesus' transfiguration as Two Witnesses, we are told. Today, Jesus and his mother appear to us in our own time with great frequency and urgency to remind us of their own words and warnings. Jesus gives us the completed picture of God's law, which we only had a partial understanding of before. It is the law of love. God's law *is* love, because God is love. His mother warns us, like any good mother, of the consequences of falling away from this law. Yes, Jesus and his mother are the Two Primary Witnesses. The two lampstands who burn with holy fire before the Lord of the World, the book of Revelation says. Don't forget, not only Mary but also Jesus is *human.* The Two Witnesses must be two *people.* But aren't there other witnesses as well, other people, who are passing on these words of warnings? Father

Bill, for example, with his feverish work to solve the puzzle of the identity of the Two Witnesses, to understand their warning which causes such consternation to the world. Your own grandmother and the hours of labor she spent to bring these Two Witnesses and their Messages to life on canvas." Sister Pen glanced briefly at Chanya, who was deep in conversation with Ajahn Preecha. She returned her gaze to Cornelia. "Perhaps there are others, too, who have been anointed as witnesses."

"You and your topiary," Cornelia said with a smile.

Sister Pen squeezed Cornelia's hand and gazed intently into her eyes. "Sometimes the old witnesses must make way for the new."

Cornelia paused, considering. Then she repeated her grand-mother's own words about her paintings. *"Satanic Christmas* reveals the identity of the Two Witnesses. *Apocalypse* reveals their message, their Warning to the World." Cornelia winced, and her shoulders sagged. *"Apocalypse* was stolen and has never been recovered. How will we ever know now—"

"Welcome, everyone, it's time to get started," a voice boomed over a microphone at the head table.

As the program commenced, a wave of dishes began to arrive for the guests to savor, including *tom yam* shrimp soup, *yam yai* salad, red curry with roasted duck, and garlic-chili trout baked in banana leaves. Cornelia was pleased that the Power Point presentation she and Chanya had labored over made such a good impression on the admiring crowd. She was a little embarrassed to see herself pop up in so many pictures and always, she realized, smiling. She was also acutely aware every time a picture appeared in which she and Chanya worked side by side. Here they were teaching English, while there they were delivering infant formula and rice to a struggling family. Here they were serving a dinner of green coconut curry and rice to the orphans, while there they were huddled together after hours going over the books. While Cornelia was inevitably smiling, Chanya's face usually had a quiet intensity about it, a kind of dogged determination. In the photos, his tan face often had a red tint, from physical exertion, possibly, or from the turmoil in his burning heart.

Sister Pen had only a short, simple slide show using antiquated equipment which stalled a time or two, including a somewhat blurred black-and-white photo of herself as a young novice nun. Cornelia tried to reconcile the stiff, conservative posture of the young Sister Pen with the cult member who had created outrageous sculptures while desperately in love with Brother Lek. Cornelia squinted and tried to see Sister Pen's features more clearly in the photo. Chanya rose to his feet and gave Sister Pen the longest and most enthusiastic applause. Ajahn Preecha did not present pictures at all, but did give a lengthy talk on the importance of involving Thai young people in the philosophy and practice of Buddhism.

Once the presentations and awards were over, and everyone had sated themselves with sticky rice and mangoes, the crowd began to disperse throughout the house and garden, sipping after-dinner coffee and chatting.

Cornelia had lost sight of Chanya at the end of the program as he was swarmed by well-wishers and potential benefactors with questions and congratulations. At one point Cornelia caught a glimpse of Sister Pen standing across the room staring fixedly at her. Or was she staring at something else? As always, the light glittering on Sister Pen's thick lenses made it hard to see her eyes. Cornelia turned and saw their hostess, Nan, introducing Ajahn Preecha to another Foundation member. Chanya was speaking earnestly with Nan's husband, Khun Boon-Mee.

After wandering down a short hall in search of a restroom, Cornelia turned a corner and found herself alone in a cozy library lined with three walls of books from floor to ceiling. The fourth wall, which included the door Cornelia had just entered through, was not covered by bookshelves, but dotted with a haphazard mixture of wall decor. A few framed ancient Thai texts hung on the wall, their frail and brittle pages behind glass. Gold-on-lacquer paintings of the Buddha hung alongside teak relief panels of elephants and serpents. Sprinkled in the midst of all these was the random family photo. Cornelia had just decided to browse the books when her cell phone vibrated. The text was from a number she didn't recognize.

BE CAREFUL. SHE IS THE ONE WHO MURDERED VIC AND TRIED TO KILL ME. I AM AWAKE NOW. I REMEMBER EVERYTHING.

Although he hadn't identified himself, Cornelia knew the text had to come from Father Bill. He had still been sedated in the hospital and unable to receive visitors when Cornelia and Chanya had departed for Bangkok, but obviously he was recovering. Cornelia had left a scrawled note for Father Bill by his hospital bed, letting him know that she and Chanya were attending today's Enlightenment Trust reception but that they would be in touch with him soon. What was it Father Bill had said when they'd arrived at his house and found him collapsed? He'd mentioned that someone had come to share tea with him. Now, thanks to Father Bill's text message, Cornelia knew it was a woman. A woman Father Bill hadn't even bothered to name, because he was so sure Cornelia would understand. She felt the first stirring of uneasiness, recalling Sister Pen's unreadable expression from across the room earlier that evening.

What had Sister Pen said to Cornelia earlier that evening? *There may be others who are anointed as witnesses.* Sister Pen had stared at both her and Chanya in the strangest way. *Sometimes the old must make way for the young.* Cornelia recalled what Old Boonsoam had said about the sculptures in the Stone Garden: *They had a strange energy.* Sculptures attributed to Brother Lek, but which in fact were the creation of Sister Pen. Cornelia recalled the faraway look in

Sister Pen's eyes when she had reminisced about her sculptures in the convent chapel. Cornelia thought again of the photograph of the stoic young Sister Pen in the slide show. What if Sister Pen had never fallen out of love with Brother Lek, had never gotten over him? Hadn't she said that her father had rescued her from Brother Lek? Maybe her father had actually forced her out of the cult and into the convent against her wishes. Sister Pen's repressed love may have led to the manic creation of the topiary of Two Witnesses— representing *Brother Lek and Sister Pen herself.* But inadvertently, she had drawn Chanya's attention to Brother Lek. Or was it deliberate? Sister Pen and Chanya had remained in touch. He would have written her, even sent her pictures of his work alongside Cornelia. He always went to visit her when he was in Laos. What if Sister Pen meant to use the topiary to lure both Chanya and Cornelia to the Stone Garden? In her undying love for Brother Lek, what if Sister Pen saw Chanya and Cornelia as the Two *New* Witnesses who would replace old Brother Lek and Sister Pen, who had been forcibly separated so many years before?

With a chill, Cornelia remembered Father Bill's unsettling question: *Who stole Satanic Christmas the second time?* After pondering that question carefully, Father Bill must have realized it could only have been Sister Pen. Sister Pen knew Father Bill and knew from him about the Twin Paintings. He could have told Sister Pen when *Satanic Christmas* was stolen from him. After Cornelia found it in Bangkok and bought it, Chanya might very well have told Sister Pen that he was keeping *Satanic Christmas* safe for Cornelia when she went to the U.S. Sister Pen could have stolen it while Chanya was out working in the slum, or simply paid one of the slum dwellers to steal it and deliver it to her. After all, she had worked in the slum for years and still had contacts there. Maybe Father Bill, after piecing all this together, had contacted Sister Pen to confront her. He surely never dreamed the diminutive nun would try to kill him. It would have been no problem for Sister Pen, a Thai citizen, to cross back into Thailand across the Mekong. It would not have been unusual for a Catholic nun to visit a Catholic priest, under the ruse of confession or spiritual counseling. Sister Pen could easily have arrived at Father Bill's door, put poison in his drink, and returned to the convent. Maybe she even used a trusting soul like Pin-Pon to help her cross the river to avoid visa stamps and a record of her journey.

That wasn't all. Since Sister Pen was in contact with Chanya, she might also have learned from him that Vic had stolen *Apocalypse* from Cornelia while she was in the States. Sister Pen could have been the woman on the night train who disguised herself and was mistaken for a *farang* by a biased Thai witness who blamed a foreigner. Sister Pen could have killed Vic and retrieved *Apocalypse*. But why? Maybe Sister Pen had wanted the paintings to confirm her insane vision of the Two Witnesses: first Brother Lek and Sister Pen, and now the mantle passed on to her beloved Chanya and the only woman in Chanya's life—Cornelia. On the other hand, Sister Pen had seen *Satanic Christmas* hanging on the wall at Father Bill's house, and he had even told her who he believed the Two Witnesses were. Maybe Sister Pen recognized that the famous paintings would destroy Brother Lek's claim to be one of the Witnesses, and she simply wanted them out of the way.

What had Sister Pen said earlier about Father Bill? In the silence of the library, the words rang in Cornelia's mind: *Rest his soul.* Sister Pen didn't realize he had recovered. The one thing she couldn't know was that Father Bill had warned Cornelia.

"Ah, you've discovered my favorite hide-out!"

Cornelia spun and found herself face to face with Chanya, Ajahn Preecha, and their wealthy Thai host, Khun Boon-Mee.

Khun Boon-Mee stood between Chanya and Ajahn Preecha and clapped a hand on each man's back. "I'm taking my two splendid friends on a tour of my house. This is where I keep my collection of Theravada texts. My two friends are most welcome to borrow them at any time." Khun Boon-Mee leaned toward Cornelia and exhaled a cloud of liquor-scented breath. "Chanya and I are going to visit Ajahn Preecha on his island. Isn't that right, my friends?"

Chanya nodded and smiled, but looked stressed. Cornelia felt like he was wilting under the pressure of performing for his benefactors. Ajahn Preecha had moved to the wall where the pages of antique Thai text hung. He peered closely to read one of the pages and began to chuckle.

Khun Boon-Mee leaned forward, weaving slightly, and frowned. "Ah!" he cried. "An old family recipe passed down through the generations. A conversation piece, of no real value."

Ajahn Preecha chortled merrily. "Wouldn't want to drink it, though."

Khun Boon-Mee barked out a laugh, but then frowned again, still weaving. "It would certainly be serious if someone were to actually use it. I believe it was meant to curse others with, although it was possibly medicinal in the tiniest of amounts. It would cause hallucinations, unconsciousness, even..." he briefly hesitated. "Death. If too much were ingested. Or the victim were particularly weak or susceptible in some way. Not to be trifled with."

Ajahn Preecha laughed uproariously. "A recipe for Thai dragon pepper potion? What will they think of next? No, not to be trifled with!"

Both Chanya and Cornelia stared at the framed, yellowed sheet covered with faint, spidery Thai writing which hung on the library wall. Cornelia looked toward Chanya, but Khun Boon-Mee had an arm hooked around his two guests' necks and was dragging them from the room. Chanya glanced back at Cornelia helplessly.

"Now I'm about to show you my *real* treasures," Khun Boon-Mee cried heartily. "I never show these to anyone." He made a dismissive gesture as they left the library. "That was nothing!"

Cornelia stood, unmoving, in the library, trying to absorb this new revelation. Boon-Mee and Nan (Rotham) Pornpipatpong had an old family recipe of a deadly dragon pepper potion hanging on their wall. Was it merely a coincidence? Cornelia's gaze drifted to the next item hanging on the wall. It was a photograph of a stiff, unsmiling young Khun Boon-Mee and a beaming Nan Rotham looking stunning in a red silk *sarong* and white blouse. Next to Nan stood a slovenly young male *farang* with long brown hair parted in the middle, clad in ragged bell-bottom blue jeans and a tight-fitting T-shirt. The T-shirt showed several people silhouetted by the sun. Above the image were the words, *The Doors*. Below the picture, *Waiting for the Sun*. The photograph looked familiar. Where had Cornelia seen it before?

"My brother was visiting us from the States," Nan said from the doorway. "I had just completed my post-college two-year volunteer stint working with the tribal people in the north. Boon was a young businessman following in his father's footsteps. We met at a soiree when I was on leave in Bangkok. When that picture was taken, we had just become engaged."

Cornelia scrutinized the photo more closely. "That's your brother?" She immediately regretted her words. Nan had just shared a pivotal moment in her life story, and Cornelia had focused only on Nan's visiting hippie brother. But she couldn't help herself. Cornelia knew now where she had seen this photograph before. Sitting on the dresser in Brother Lek's cramped little room, his "temple." Cornelia was certain that she was looking at Brother Lek, fifty years younger, with hair.

"And the irony is he never left," Nan murmured. "He's still here. I've always felt responsible for him, and he's always depended on me." She sighed and then seemed to catch herself, turning and facing Cornelia with a benign hostess expression. "I wondered where you and your handsome co-worker had got off to." She glanced around the empty library, faintly puzzled. "Where is he?"

"Oh, your husband was taking him and Ajahn Preecha to see something," Cornelia said carelessly.

Almost imperceptibly, Nan tensed. "To see what?" she asked, giving Cornelia a forced *fun yim* smile.

Cornelia swallowed. Nan was blocking her only exit from the room. She was taller than Cornelia, but Cornelia was much younger and much stronger.

"I don't know," Cornelia said truthfully. "Treasures. He said he was going to show them his real treasures."

Anger flared in Nan's eyes as she swiveled on her heels and strode briskly away. At that moment Cornelia's phone vibrated again. This time it was a call, not a text, and Cornelia recognized the number.

"Yes. Father Bill," Cornelia said in a low voice. "I'm in Nan's home. I've found the recipe she used to poison you."

"Cornelia! Thank God you're all right. As soon as I woke up and read your note, about a reception at her house, it all came together."

"Why did she try to kill you?"

"I invited her," Father Bill replied glumly. "I saw her on the night train and invited her to stop by my house the next day for tea. She told me she had come to town to attend a ribbon-cutting at a new jobs center the Enlightenment Trust was funding. A limousine was waiting for her at the train station." Father Bill paused. "She always flew. She never took the train. I remember thinking how unusual it was to see her there. We were both American ex-pats who had been living in Thailand for years. Of course I knew her. I knew Brother Lek was her wayward missing brother. I wanted to warn her that he was in real trouble this time, finally going off the deep end. She arrived at my house that afternoon, after you had left. She thanked me for my concern. She seemed distant, but..." He was silent for a moment. "Then I told her I felt obligated to go to the police with my concerns about her brother. I told her I was concerned he was involved in the theft of some paintings, and Vic's murder on the night train. As soon as I said it, I remembered the police telling me about a foreign woman seen on the night train. Up until that instant, I had dismissed the report as being about *you*. But I stood face-to-face with her that night in my house, and realized it had been Nan herself who had been on the night train to steal *Apocalypse*."

"And to kill Vic," Cornelia reminded him.

"It may have been accidental," Father Bill said slowly. "I'll wager she was just trying to knock him out for a while. Spike his drink and take the painting as soon as he was unconscious. She might have pretended to be surprised to see him on the train. Or maybe he'd arranged to meet with her about buying the painting. Vic probably called Brother Lek right after he stole *Satanic Christmas* from me. Vic had been coming over and having coffee with me and looking at that painting. He knew Brother Lek would be interested. He probably called Brother Lek at the Garden of Ghosts and they wouldn't let him speak to their leader immediately."

"He was probably meditating," Cornelia agreed. "Or pretending to."

"Vic was forced to leave a message for him. I suspect that Vic panicked, frightened of getting caught and dying in a Thai prison, so he bolted instead of waiting to hear back from Brother Lek. He was just a desperate man, you know, not a professional criminal. He got rid of the painting in Bangkok as fast as he could and caught a plane to the U.S. He wanted to get away from the people who were after him for his debts."

"Yes, and while he was selling *Satanic Christmas* in the Bangkok shop and planning to flee to the U.S., he got the idea of tracking down *Apocalypse* once he was in America," Cornelia suggested. "I remember that the clerk said Vic had discussed the second painting with him, and how much it would be worth."

"I'm afraid I put that idea in his head," Father Bill said regretfully. "He knew about my efforts to locate the twin painting, *Apocalypse*. We had talked about it, occasionally, over the years.

This whole sad episode of him stealing both *Satanic Christmas* and *Apocalypse* was his rather botched attempt at getting himself out of his gambling debts."

"That would also explain why Nan showed up in the Bangkok shop wanting to buy the painting," Cornelia said. "Her brother had contacted her about the message from Vic, the chance to get *Satanic Christmas*. Maybe she had called Vic back, and he told her he'd already sold it to the shop. That's how she knew where to find it. But her questions spooked the clerk, made him wonder if it was stolen, which, of course, it was. She was probably trying to intimidate him with her questions about the *provenance,* letting him know that she knew it was stolen, and he'd better hand it over. But her bullying backfired, scared him off. He told her to come back later." Cornelia reflected. "That's the only reason I found *Satanic Christmas* again. It's the only reason I went home and learned the truth about my grandmother and the Twin Paintings."

"If only Vic had gone back to the U.S. and stayed there," Father Bill lamented. "Instead he started thinking about *Apocalypse* and got greedy. He returned to Thailand and probably offered to sell *Apocalypse* to Nan and Brother Lek for a formidable sum—enough to get Vic out of his gambling debts and ensure he could comfortably live out his days in his house in Thailand."

"Why didn't he sell it in the U.S. where it would fetch a much higher price?" Cornelia wondered aloud.

"Too much heat," Father Bill suggested. "Recently reported stolen, and too many experts who would recognize the painting's value if he tried to put it up for sale. A much higher chance of getting caught. Better to sell in a foreign land, under the table, to someone with his own shady agenda. But the price was too high. Nan offered him a spiked drink instead and unintentionally killed him." Father Bill sighed. "I think it was the same with me. She came still carrying her potion, her poison left over from Vic on the night train. But she only decided to use it on me when she realized I was going to go to the police and that I knew she herself might be involved in Vic's murder. In my case, my phone rang, and when I took the call, from a parishioner, that's when she poisoned the tea."

"It's strange," Cornelia said thoughtfully. "Brother Lek appeared to die in front of his all his followers. They thought he was dead. He looked dead. They had a huge blow-up photograph of him seemingly dead. I wonder if he had taken some of his sister's potion to render himself convincingly unconscious."

"Quite possible," Father Bill said. "They had an unhealthy and dysfunctional relationship. Nan coddled her little brother and enabled him in his delusions. I think it came from a difficult childhood. Nan never spoke of the details. It wouldn't surprise me if she had whipped up a batch of her potion to assist Brother Lek in his charade of dying and rising again."

"Her little brother," Cornelia repeated. "Little Brother. Brother Lek. That's probably where his name came from. Did Nan consider herself the Second Witness?" Cornelia asked. "Did she want the two paintings to glorify herself and her brother as the Two Witnesses, or did she want to hide them because they ruined Brother Lek's claim?"

"Nan Rotham did not think she was a Second Witness," Father Bill snorted. "But she most certainly may have stolen the paintings for her brother. He wanted them because he was delusional and thought he was one of the Witnesses. Nan probably saw an added benefit due to their monetary value. There *have* been rumors that her husband's business ventures are not doing well." Father Bill took a deep breath and continued. "Nan failed to get *Satanic Christmas* for her little brother from Vic. She wasn't going to miss again. I doubt Nan went into the slum and stole *Satanic Christmas* from Chanya's office, but she certainly could have paid someone to do so."

"The shop clerk told me she was coming back again, with her husband, to buy *Satanic Christmas*. When she went back, someone in the shop probably told Nan who bought it." Cornelia hesitated. "I used a credit card. A little bribe, or a little pressure from the powerful Khun Boon Mee, and Nan could have found out my identity easily enough."

"Ah," Father Bill said. "That explains a missing piece. Your name, a private detective, an inquiry here or there. Nan could easily have discovered what this young American woman was doing in Thailand and where she was working. And it just so happened that you worked in the very same slum project which was about to be honored by a Foundation her husband was involved in. She was able to learn all about both you and Chanya, and where *Satanic Christmas* might be."

"And there weren't that many places to look," Cornelia pointed out. "My apartment. Chanya's office. He just keeps a cot in the backroom. He doesn't even have his own place."

"Nan made sure the painting was delivered to Brother Lek where she *knew* he would keep it safe because of his own personal fantasies," Father Bill noted. "After all, it's an extremely difficult painting to de-code. Brother Lek may have honestly believed the painting pointed toward *him* as one of the witnesses."

"He did sort of see himself as Jesus," Cornelia agreed. "But there's something else. When I found it in his room, it was set up on an easel, and there were jars of paint there. It's also possible that he was planning to change it, enhance it to try to prove *he* was one of the Two Witnesses. And in the end, he was willing to let it perish in the flames rather than allow us to escape with it and disprove his claim."

"In any case, Nan believed *Satanic Christmas* was safely hidden away in Laos until she decided she needed to sell it. When Brother Lek told her that Vic now had the second painting to sell, she understood that owning both of them would increase the paintings' value exponentially. She killed the first time accidentally for *Apocalypse* because she misjudged the amount of potion she should give Vic, or because of Vic's general poor health. The drugging was pre-meditated, but not the murder. She tried to kill a second time only because I was going to the police about her brother's involvement in the thefts and the murder. And she realized I was beginning to suspect her, too." Father Bill sighed, sounding sorrowful. "It was a crime of opportunity, but she did intend to murder me."

"Have you reported her to the police? That she tried to kill you?" Cornelia asked.

"Not yet," Father Bill said. He coughed. "Don't forget I just woke up in a hospital bed, and after I read your note, my first thought was to warn you. I doubt there will be proof of murder, though. It just looks like I over-indulged in dragon peppers."

Cornelia frowned. "You may be right. Someone had washed the tea kettle and cups in your house. They were drying on the draining board." She brightened. "But the recipe is hanging right here on the wall. And that's not all. Brother Lek gave Chanya a small bottle of potion which he was supposed to administer to me." Cornelia laughed nervously. "To kill me with. I'll bet someone with expertise could analyze it and see if it matches this recipe. Hold on, Father Bill. I'm going to take a picture of the recipe with my phone."

"Good idea," Father Bill said. "Can I talk to Chanya?"

"No," Cornelia said. "He went with Ajahn Preecha and Nan's husband to look at some treasures he had."

"You mean you and Chanya are separated? You're in the house alone? And so is he?" Father Bill's voice was tense. "I thought you were together. I was going to tell you to leave as soon as Chanya received his award. After all, Nan may not have started out as a murderer, but she is certainly one now. You can't predict what some people may do when they're feeling cornered and desperate. And Nan could be feeling cornered and desperate with you and Chanya in her house. She knows who you are, of course. But she doesn't know that you have figured out who *she* is."

Cornelia recalled her shocked words to Nan: *That's your brother?* Did Nan realize that Cornelia now knew who she was? "Father Bill. I'm hanging up now and going to find Chanya. I'll be in touch."

Cornelia ran down the hallway and into the great dining room. The overhead chandeliers had been dimmed but not extinguished. The long shining teakwood tables had been cleared and were adorned simply with jasmine flowers and votive candles. Traditional Thai music tinkled soothingly over speakers. Coffee urns and pitchers of ice water were strategically situated throughout the room. Small clusters of guests were scattered about. Two elegantly-dressed Thai women stood murmuring at one end, one of them clutching her purse and jacket. The event was beginning to wind down. At the other end of the room, floor-to-ceiling wooden shutters stood open to an expansive covered porch and surrounding tropical garden. Cornelia stepped out onto the porch where wooden ceiling fans rotated languidly above rattan chairs and bamboo porch gliders.

"Just in time," Chanya said smoothly, touching Cornelia on the arm. He bowed deeply, hands folded, to his host and hostess, Khun Boon Mee and Khun Nan. Cornelia followed suit.

Khun Boon Mee offered an unsteady return bow, while Nan gave a rather careless *wai* to her departing guests.

"As I said, Chanya, I'm so sorry you weren't able to view our art collection," Nan purred in her well-modulated voice. "Some of the pieces are ancient and fragile, and the climate control system is quite delicate. If we opened it during parties, the constant in-and-out of guests would upset the atmospheric controls which are in place to safeguard the integrity of the pieces. Never mind the potential damage done by visitors breathing and perspiring. And, God forbid, if anyone should touch the pieces. But we couldn't possibly keep a constant eye on everyone, could we?"

"I understand completely," Chanya said, smiling. "It's been a pleasure. And now we'll go." He tugged at Cornelia, who grudgingly followed. She was bursting with both questions and comments, but Chanya seemed preoccupied and in a hurry. And she'd promised Father Bill they would leave as quickly as possible. Khun Boon Mee's eyes were glassy and he appeared to have given up any attempt at polite conversation.

"We do hope you'll come again," Nan said, her face neutral.

"I'm sure we'll meet again," Chanya said. Nan blinked.

Outside in the humid tropical night, Chanya and Cornelia quickly slid into the backseat of an air conditioned taxi. As soon as the car door slammed shut, Cornelia burst out, "It's her!"

"I know," Chanya agreed.

"How did you know? Father Bill called me and told me everything."

"I saw the dragon pepper recipe, for one thing. Then Khun Boon Mee took me and Ajahn Preecha on a drunken tour of his art collection."

"But Nan said—"

"She caught up with us a bit too late," Chanya said complacently. "We were just leaving the art gallery, but Nan thought we were trying to get in." Chanya chuckled. "Nan snatched the keys from Boon Mee and made sure the alarm panel was re-set. Boon Mee was too drunk to let his wife know that we'd already been in. And me—well, I had my own reasons for keeping mum on the subject."

Outside the car window, they sailed past old colonial-era homes along the Chao Praya river. Up ahead, the Hua Lamphong Train Station glowed like a mirage.

Cornelia turned and fixed her gaze on Chanya. "What reasons did you have? For keeping mum?"

"I told you. I saw their art collection."

Outside, Cornelia glimpsed the frenetic energy of Chinatown with its plucked ducks hanging in shop windows and Chinese neon signs flashing erratically.

Chanya continued. "Now I know why Khun Nan was so unwilling to show off her art collection tonight."

"*Apocalypse,*" Cornelia guessed. "After drugging Vic, she carried it off the train and into the waiting limousine and back to Bangkok." Chanya was smiling, which Cornelia didn't understand. "She's going to remove it. Probably tonight. She'll try to hide it or sell it or something. I'll never see it again." Cornelia bit her lip. "We'll never discover the message from the Two Witnesses that my grandmother painted in *Apocalypse.*"

"Oh, I think we will," Chanya said. He held up his phone. On the screen shimmered a photo of *Apocalypse* which Chanya had snapped while inside the room. On one side of the painting stood a grinning Khun Boon Mee, and on the other side a quietly smiling Ajahn Preecha.

"You see, Ajahn Preecha explained that he had no need for a cash prize," Chanya said. "He lives in a cave on an island. Devotees bring him food. He asked Khun Boon Mee if he might have a painting instead of cash for his prize," Chanya said. "Khun Boon Mee couldn't possibly turn down this world-famous Buddhist monk who had just won a huge prize. He even let Ajahn Preecha pick."

"And he picked *Apocalypse?*" Cornelia was surprised. "But there was probably valuable Thai and Buddhist art in there. Why?"

"During dinner, I had filled Ajahn Preecha in on our wild adventures," Chanya explained. "He was very impressed. He found it all highly entertaining. He has an excellent sense of humor. When the dinner hour ended, Ajahn Preecha knew as much as we did: *Satanic Christmas* was lost in a fire and *Apocalypse* had been stolen by a mysterious and seemingly dangerous character. Mystery unsolved."

"Then Ajahn Preecha saw *Apocalypse* in Khun Boon Mee's art collection," Cornelia guessed.

"Ajahn Preecha had already left by the time Nan discovered me and her husband exiting the art collection," Chanya said. "Ajahn Preecha keeps monk's hours, of course. Early to bed, and all that. He had jumped in a taxi with his new painting and sped on his way to the Bangkok *wat* where he will spend the night." Chanya cleared his throat. "In fact, he invited me to stop by that very *wat* tonight on our way home."

Cornelia stared from Chanya's phone to his face. If anyone had been watching, they would have seen a rare sight: A stunned, serious, unsmiling Cornelia and a beaming Chanya, each looking deeply into the other's eyes.

Cornelia spoke first, still not smiling. "I got some other good news tonight."

"What was that?" Chanya asked.

"Brother Lek isn't my grandfather."

"That *is* good news," Chanya agreed. He was silent a moment. "Do you think he survived the fire?"

"Who knows? His sister talked about him tonight as if he was still alive. *He's still here*, she said." Cornelia sighed, and allowed herself to rest her head on Chanya's broad shoulder. "What matters is that we're still on the trail of *Apocalypse*."

Chanya took Cornelia's hand tenderly in his own, still smiling. "We're still on the trail."

ABOUT THE AUTHOR

L. R. Walker has taught ESL in Thailand and worked as a journalist. The Twin Paintings Mystery is the first novel in Walker's Strange Islands Mystery series. Walker is also the author of a nonfiction book, The Mystery of Garabandal: Fantasy or Fraud? Ghost or God?